MW00586769

The Cryptic Cold Case

A 1920s historical mystery

A Dora and Rex Mystery
Book 6

Lynn Morrison

Marketing Chair Press

Copyright © 2024 by Lynn Morrison

All rights reserved.

No part of this book may be reproduced in any form or by any electronic or mechanical means, including information storage and retrieval systems, without written permission from the author, except for the use of brief quotations in a book review.

This novel's story and characters are fictitious. Certain long-standing institutions, agencies, and public offices are mentioned, but the story are wholly imaginary. Some of the characters were inspired by actual historical figures, and abide by the generally known facts about these individuals and their relevant time periods. However, their actions and conversations are strictly fiction. All other characters and events are the product of my own imagination.

Cover design by DLR Cover Designs

Published by

The Marketing Chair Press, Oxford, England

LynnMorrisonWriter.com

Print ISBN: 978-1-7392632-7-0

Chapter 1
A Dinner of Discovery

Although etiquette strictly prohibited fisticuffs at dinner, wars of words were deemed acceptable. It was for that reason that Dora had insisted on inviting Lord Audley to their weekly family dinner.

As usual, Lady Edith, the Dowager Duchess of Rockingham and Rex's grandmother, played hostess, claiming the seat at one end of the table. Rex's sister, Caledonia, and Dora's brother, Benedict, sat on her left and right.

Rex sat opposite his grandmother, with Dora and her mother flanking his sides. That left two empty seats in the centre. It was no accident that Dora's father, Lord Cavendish, and her mentor, Lord Audley found themselves seated opposite one another.

The august pair of political leaders had been arch-rivals since their prep school days. Adulthood, marriage, and children had done little to temper their relationship. When one stated an opinion, the other argued the opposite. Once, they'd spent half an hour engaging in a heated debate over the proper way to pronounce "scone".

Lord Audley insisted it rhymed with "cone," passionately

arguing that this pronunciation was the hallmark of true sophistication and class. Lord Cavendish vehemently stated it should rhyme with "gone," citing obscure historical texts and the practices of ancient British tea rooms as irrefutable evidence of his stance. Their argument escalated to where they were consulting dusty old dictionaries in the Westminster library and recruiting opinions from bewildered clerks who chanced upon the pair. Only the call to session prevented them from carrying on until dark.

Simply put, there was little the men loved more than casting aspersions on the other. They had plenty of reasons to make peace, yet they never let bygones be bygones. The fact of the matter was that they enjoyed their rivalry far too much to let it drop.

When Dora once asked her father why he carried on, he made a confession. "My debates with Lord Audley keep me sharp. Should the day come when I can no longer hold my own against him, I will know it is time to hang up my hat and retreat to the countryside. Although he'll never admit it, I am sure he feels the same."

Lately, however, Lord Audley seemed out of sorts. Dora caught him gazing off into the distance during one of her longer updates. He'd been late to a meeting, and had forgotten another. Either his mind was elsewhere, or the years were taking their toll. Given he was barely half a century old, Dora sincerely hoped it was the former and not the latter.

She wouldn't rest until she was sure.

Thus, with the dowager's permission, Dora had arranged for tonight's dinner to be a test.

With a possible general election looming on the horizon, Dora had been sure the men would rise to the occasion. Her father, a staunch conservative, loved to expound upon his party's chance to entrench their hold on power. As a crossbencher with no affiliation, Lord Audley should have rushed to highlight the party's flaws. The resulting argument would easily carry them through from appetiser to dessert.

That was, however, if all was well with Lord Audley.

Rex's grandmother raised the topic of conversation early on, asking Lord Cavendish whether he thought Prime Minister Baldwin would dissolve parliament. While Dora's father waxed on about mandates and tariffs, Dora's gaze remained fixed on Lord Audley's face.

Things started well enough. Lord Cavendish put his stake in the ground. Lord Audley promptly took the opposite. Dora's fears evaporated as the men battled in their game of one-upmanship.

But then Dora's brother Benedict waded into the fray, espousing the viewpoint of the younger generation. Rex laughed at his ivory tower view and suggested he spend more time walking with the common man. When the other guests joined the conversation, Lord Audley once again got that far-off expression on his face. Dora worried in earnest when her father outright won a point in their friendly debate.

Knowing she had to take action and doing so were far different things. One didn't make demands of Lord Audley. Even Dora, notorious for winding him up, held back from prying into his private matters.

But if some situation was bad enough to occupy this much of Lord Audley's attention, Dora had little choice but to act.

When Rex's grandmother suggested they retire to the drawing room for after-dinner drinks, Dora excused herself. She needed a moment alone to decide which tactic to take. Should she confront Lord Audley now, while she had her family to echo her concern?

Logic argued it was better to wait until they were on their own. But waiting didn't sit right with Dora, either.

She stepped into the nearest powder room and stared into the eyes of her reflection. A soft rap on the door distracted her before she reached a decision.

"Dora, it's me," her mother murmured. "Open up."

Dora flipped the lock and opened the door.

"Step back so I can come in."

With a raised brow, Dora did as her mother ordered. Lady Adaline locked the door behind herself and then faced her daughter. Although their hair and eye colours did not match, they bore the same upturned noses and full lips.

Right now, Lady Adaline's lips were pursed into a frown. "What is wrong with Audley? He isn't himself."

"Drat," Dora muttered. "So you've noticed as well."

"Your father's crowed twice this week about getting something past his rival. After tonight, I'm certain it isn't due to Stephen's prowess, no matter what he claims. Is there something we need to know? Something we can do?"

"I haven't a clue, Mama, but I'll be sure to tell you when I do. To be honest, it is reassuring to know I can count upon your aid." Dora gave her mother a hug, letting the fresh floral notes of her mother's perfume fill her nose. She'd worn the scent for as long as Dora could remember. The delicate blend evoked memories of playing dress-up in her mother's gowns and finding safety after a bad dream.

Dora almost wished she were still a child. Her mother and father could step in and right the wrongs in her world. But childhood days were far behind her. As a married woman and professional spy, she had to fight her own battles.

That thought led to another until Dora came to a decision. She'd wait until the next day to force Lord Audley to submit to her inquisition. In private, he was far more likely to come clean.

Now resolved, Dora pulled free of her mother's embrace.

"We'd better get back to the others before Edith sends out a search party."

Lady Adaline caught Dora's hands and gave them a gentle squeeze. "I can't tell you how delighted I am that you and Edith have forged a strong bond. It almost makes up for you and Rex getting married in secret. I still cannot believe it was unplanned."

"Trust me, Mama, even I didn't know it was coming. If you want to have words with anyone, you'll have to come visit Inga. She's the one who pulled the strings."

Dora's mother patted her on the cheek. "The only words I have for Inga are thank you. Edith and I hoped you and Rex would one day settle down, but I expected we would have to threaten you two to get you to the altar. Given your propensity to flout society, we'll take what we can get, even if it means we missed the big event."

They freshened their lipstick and hurried to the drawing room. As was often the case, the group had broken apart, with the men smoking cigars on one end and the women chatting on the other. Dora left the men to their discussion of racing odds and followed her mother across the room. She was happy to enjoy a rare moment to shed her image as a French femme fatale and simply play the role of dutiful daughter and wife.

Rex's grandmother sat in her usual velvet upholstered wingback chair, with Caledonia beside her. They smiled at the women and beckoned them over. Sheffield, the dowager's butler, served Dora and her mother glasses of Port.

Now comfortable, Dora's mother asked Caledonia how her musical studies were progressing.

"My stay in Rome allowed me to make significant progress in understanding Verdi. There was a cultural aspect I struggled to grasp from books alone."

"Is he a favourite of yours?" Lady Adaline asked.

"Yes, but one of many, I'm afraid. My tutors suggest I narrow my focus with the intention of becoming an expert on a single composer."

"You disagree?"

Caledonia shrugged her shoulders. "The thing I love most about my studies is the challenge. I fear that if I specialise, I'll grow bored."

"Darling girl, you will never be bored. You're simply too strong-willed to accept such a situation," Edith said. "Be honest with us. You have some little side project on the go, haven't you? Some puzzle you're piecing together. Perhaps one that might explain why you have been covered in dust all week."

"And here I thought you had not noticed..." Caledonia wrinkled her nose as her cheeks pinked. "I found the most interesting trunk in the depths of the attic."

"The attic?" Dora was certain she had misheard. "Whatever were you doing up there?"

"It is a veritable treasure trove of family history," Caledonia explained. "We could organise a museum display with the period clothing alone. I went up in search of old family diaries, interested to see if I could find references to attending debuts and concerts of some of the older composers. You would be amazed at how much the cultural context can help with interpreting an artist's work."

"Well, did you find anything?" Lady Edith asked. "Do not leave us in suspense."

Caledonia bobbed her head at her grandmother. "I was going to tell you about it later, but I suppose there's no harm in sharing it now. I chanced upon an old trunk, dating back to around a century ago. There are diaries, letters, and even encrypted messages."

"Really?" Lady Edith arched one perfectly shaped eyebrow.

She motioned for Caledonia to continue her explanation. "How did they end up here?"

"They must have belonged to some relative of ours. I have only just begun to explore what is stored in the trunk, Grandma. I am cataloguing the contents first, and then will work on identifying all the people. From there, it should be simple enough to figure out which one of them is in our extended family tree."

"What of the messages written in code?" Dora asked. "Will you send them to a specialist for decryption?"

"Oh no," Caledonia brushed the question aside. "I can do that part myself."

Lady Edith, Dora, and Dora's mother sat up straight and goggled at Caledonia. Was there anything the clever girl could not do? Decrypting century-old letters was a far different task than studying music scores and reading history books. Even Dora, versatile and specially trained as she was, would struggle to unravel the secrets contained within the notes. Never mind that such desk-bound tasks had never been her favourites.

Edith asked Caledonia how she planned to accomplish the task, but Dora put a hand up before she replied.

"Rex," Dora called loud enough to catch her husband's attention. "All of you, actually. You must come and listen to what Caledonia is planning. I'm sure you'll all be equally intrigued."

Rex rested his handmade Cuban cigar on the edge of a nearby ashtray and motioned for the others to follow. They'd all spent enough time in Edith's company to know she had little tolerance for the habit.

Dora scooted over and patted the space on the upholstered sofa. Rex abided by her silent command and settled beside her. The other men availed themselves of the remaining nearby chairs.

"Your sister was telling us she discovered a trove of diaries and letters, including some written in code, in the attic. If that is not interesting enough, she's told us of her plans to go a step further and decipher the encrypted letters."

Rex reacted as Dora expected, rocking sideways in shock. Every new piece of information about his sister sent him reeling.

"How the deuce will you manage that?" Rex asked. "What other skills are you hiding away?"

Caledonia rolled her eyes at her brother. "I'm not hiding anything. It's your fault for so rarely coming home. As for the decryption, I discovered it as a child. I was always desperate for new puzzles. A tutor handed me a book on encoding techniques throughout history and suggested I turn my mind to that. These diary entries should not be that difficult."

"Easy for you to say," Dora murmured, giving Caledonia a wink. "I'd say they're all Greek to me, but I studied Greek at school. The few coded messages I've seen always look as though someone threw the alphabet into the air and wrote the letters in the order they landed."

"It's a little more scientific than that, Dora," Benedict said, always ready to correct his sister. "Caledonia, please carry on. Do you know to whom the diaries and letters belong?"

Rex's sister leaned forward and lowered her voice. "The writer of at least one of them was a young woman named Grace, and the entries start with her arrival in London for her first Season."

Benedict pulled a face, causing Dora to laugh aloud. "That's disappointing."

"Not in the least. This young woman had a dry wit and keen intelligence. The entries are far from lists of daily activities or meals eaten."

While Caledonia shared more of her discovery, Dora

allowed her gaze to drift around the room. It landed squarely on the face of Lord Audley.

For the first time since her return from Rome, Lord Audley was giving his full attention. The rapt expression on his face was echoed in his posture. Dora could practically see the calculations running through his mind.

Was it simply the joy of discovering a skilled code-breaker living in their midst? Or did Lord Audley have a specific assignment in mind for the talented young woman?

Those questions swirled through Dora's thoughts, unanswered, until it was time for everyone to go. Still determined to have a quiet word with her mentor, Dora offered to see Lord Audley out.

Before she could ask if he had a free space in his busy diary, he surprised her by asking the same.

"Can you and Rex come to my house tomorrow? Say four in the afternoon? I have a new case for you to investigate."

Dora tamped down the thrill of excitement that always accompanied those words. A new case didn't necessarily mean she'd get answers to the questions on her mind. "Of course. Can you give me any hints?"

Lord Audley glanced around to make sure there was no one within earshot. The only person in the corridor was the butler, and he stood waiting at the other end, next to the front door.

"It's a personal matter, so I must ask for your discretion." Lord Audley lowered his voice to barely more than a whisper. "I have reason to believe my wife's death twenty-five years ago wasn't an accident."

Chapter 2
Audley's Secret

R ex loved riding the London underground. If it weren't for
Dora, he'd never have discovered it. He was aware of its
existence, of course, but men of his set travelled almost
exclusively by Rolls-Royce or some other similarly expensive
model.

In his early days of training, Dora had pointed out that the
working class could hardly afford such luxury. When disguised
as servants, clerks, or tradesmen, they had to travel by means
appropriate to their station.

For most Londoners, that was the Tube.

Today, dressed in secondhand clothes and wigs, Rex and
Dora descended the stairs to the platform. The hustle and
bustle of London's busy streets followed them, albeit at a more
sedate pace. An underlying hum of anticipation accompanied
the chorus of footsteps, the rustle of newspapers, and the
occasional sharp whistle that sliced through the cacophony. The
aroma of strong tobacco smoke mingled with the oily scent of
machinery, a reminder of the industrial prowess that powered
these subterranean carriages.

On the train, Rex and Dora lucked into empty seats on the

wooden benches polished by wear. Rex had a copy of the day's paper tucked under his arm. He'd bought it for a few coins from a boy calling to passersby outside the station. Rex had already read it, but that was no matter. Now, it served another purpose. He opened the paper and lifted it until it covered his face. Surreptitiously, he peered over the top of the pages, studying the faces of his fellow riders.

He'd discovered he could learn much from studying his fellow travellers, noticing their expressions, mannerisms, and clothing. Each trip allowed him to improve his own disguises. Today's trip was too short for him to learn much. All too soon, they arrived at the Bond Street station. Despite the sweat dotting his brow and the rank stench of unwashed bodies, Rex was loath to return above ground.

Up there, under the cloudy sky, reality waited.

"Chin up," Dora said while latching onto his arm. "Whatever else, this day is highly unlikely to be boring."

The reminder perked Rex up. Audley's parting remark the evening before had left Dora with her mouth agape. On their ride home, the newlyweds took turns guessing what he might have meant. They ended up no further along than when they'd started.

Dora and Rex had been children in the nursery when Lady Audley died. Why would Lord Audley think her death was anything but an accident? Especially now?

At the very least, Rex and Dora now knew why Audley had been out of sorts. As to what they'd be able to do about it, that remained to be seen.

The couple entered Audley's London mansion through the servant's entrance. The butler met them in the kitchen and led them upstairs to the study, where his grace sat waiting.

Dora paused in the doorway and bobbed a curtsy. "You asked to see us, your grace?"

Audley rolled his eyes, waved them inside, and finally asked his butler to send up tea. They made polite conversation until the footman delivered the tea tray and left them alone.

Dora dropped two cubes of sugar into her cup while encouraging Lord Audley to come clean. "You can hardly dangle the word *murder* and expect us to wait patiently. What is this all about?"

Rex kept a close watch over his superior. Usually cool with an unreadable expression, today dark shadows hung from Lord Audley's eyes. He ignored the cup of tea and plate of biscuits, choosing instead to stare out the window.

Despite his request for help, Audley was still struggling with the matter.

"A burden shared is a burden halved," Rex said, prompting the older man to speak up.

Audley sighed audibly and shifted to face his guests. "The matter is simple enough. Twenty-five years ago, my wife died in a riding accident. Or, at least, so I thought."

"What changed?" Dora asked.

"While you were away, I received a note through the post. Unsigned, as is always the case. It contained a single line. *Your wife's death was no accident.*"

"I assume you investigated."

Audley nodded at Dora. "With you two away and my other agents abroad, I went through private channels. A London investigator came highly recommended."

"What did he find?"

"A cold trail and little else. Not that I expected much. He handed over his notes and said he could do no more. I tried to convince myself the note was some sort of sick joke, but the suspicion refused to fade."

Rex screwed up his face. "We're happy to help any way we

can. But if the investigator hit a wall, what makes you think we'll do any better?"

"Because of these," Audley said. He grabbed a packet of letters from his desk.

"Not more letters," Dora groaned. "This is the Prince Bertie assignment all over again."

"I almost wish that was the case. There are, however, two key differences. The first is that these letters were not addressed to me."

"And the second?" Dora asked.

"I'll get to that in a moment. First, allow me to explain how I got them. As I was saying earlier, I could not let go of the fear the anonymous note inspired. If what the sender said was true, and my wife was murdered, I must somehow be to blame."

Rex's heart stuttered at the anguish in Audley's voice. The man lived at the centre of a web of intrigue. It would only take a small mistake for danger to rip through the delicate lines.

Rex and Dora lived with this same risk. To protect her family, Dora had stayed away for four long years. She had only returned once her credentials held up under scrutiny. Rex had yet to tell his own parents any of it. Certainly, they'd have read of his relationship with Dora in the papers. But they remained unaware of his marriage and his role as an undercover spy. The less they knew, the more likely they were to remain safe in their country manor.

As for his grandmother... Heaven help anyone naïve enough to tangle with the Dowager Duchess. Between her place in society and the footmen Rex had trained to protect her, she was safe in her Mayfair fortress.

Rex drew his mind back to the present. The man sitting across from him was older and wiser. But twenty-five years was a long time. That long ago, Audley would have been at the start of his rise to be the power behind the throne.

Perhaps he had not yet built those walls of protection around his home. If so, had it cost his wife her life?

A shudder racked Rex's control. He gripped onto the armrests of his chair to keep Audley from seeing it.

He need not have bothered. Lord Audley was lost in his own memories. The letters transfixed him, proving their power.

Dora coughed lightly to get his attention. "You were telling us about the letters."

Audley blinked a few times to bring himself back to the present. "Yes. When the private investigation came up dry, I decided it was time I faced my past. I had the servants retrieve my wife's things from the attic. They'd packed them away after her death. Then, I'd had no reason to put myself through the pain of searching through them."

"The letters were hers?" Dora asked.

Lord Audley nodded. "I found them hidden in her hope chest, tucked into the folds of her wedding dress."

Rex imagined the horror Audley must have felt at discovering he wasn't the only one in his home with secrets.

Lady Audley had taken hers to the grave. Or so she'd thought...

A quarter of a century later, those secrets were under the spotlight. Yet, the shadows they made remained impenetrable.

Rex forced himself to ask the question. "What do the letters say?"

Lord Audley grimaced. "That brings us to our second point of differentiation from our previous case. Then, the sender took pains to hide their identity, but not the contents of their letters. Now, it is the opposite. The letters are written in a cypher."

"Really?" Dora shifted forward in her seat and held out a hand.

Audley passed the letters over. Dora laid them out on her lap. There were four, each one encased in a nondescript envelope bearing Lady Audley's name. There was nothing to make them stand out from the normal daily post.

"Don't get them out of order. They are undated. I am working on the assumption that she stacked them with the most recent on top."

Dora picked up the letter that from the bottom of the stack. The envelope had a neat slit in the side. She gave it a light shake and a single folded sheet of paper fell out.

They leaned closer to get a look at the contents. Several lines of jumbled letters filled half the page. There was no date, signature, or hint of a key.

"What do they say?" Rex asked.

"I'm hoping your sister can tell us," Audley replied.

Rex's gaze shot from the paper to Audley's face. "Caledonia? Surely you have more experienced code-breakers at your service. Perhaps someone who played that role during the war?"

"I cannot comment on whether the government has now or ever employed the services of a code-breaker," Audley said in a firm tone. "Suffice it to say, I have no one else whom I trust with a secret of this magnitude."

"You are assuming it is a state secret," Rex countered. "It might be as simple as an affair."

Lord Audley stiffened at Rex's suggestion. Pain flashed in his eyes. These deeds were well in the past, but the hurt remained.

Dora laid a hand on Rex's arm, reminding him to tread lightly.

"You are afraid something in here could be used against you," Dora guessed.

The older man's mouth settled in a grim line. His nostrils flared as he breathed in and released a heavy sigh. "I don't have a clue what to think. It seems ludicrous to imagine something so long ago as being relevant now."

"But it must be," Dora insisted. "Why else would someone have sent you that note? Before then, you had no hint anything was amiss, correct?"

"My wife tumbled from her horse while out for her morning ride. It may well have been an accident, this note notwithstanding. But I can't rest until I have the answer. Now that I've waded into the dark depths of my past, my only choices are to swim through or drown in the what-ifs."

Rex's stomach roiled. He could hardly turn his back on his mentor. Yet, he did not want his sister to be drawn into this life. The push and pull of these competing emotions left him feeling sick.

"This is why you've been preoccupied of late?" Dora asked.

"Can you blame me?"

Dora shook her head. She folded the paper and returned it to the envelope. Then she gathered the other three and stacked them in order. She offered the bunch to Rex. "My answer is, of course, yes. I will help however I can. But you must decide."

Rex eyed the envelopes the way he would a snake. Unfortunately, they lacked the distinctive colouring to indicate whether they were venomous. "I have no hesitation on my part. But Caledonia? She is too young."

"She is a woman grown," Dora reminded him in a gentle tone. "Older brother or not, it is not your place to answer for her."

Rex rocked back. "You'd put her at risk?"

"Not on purpose. None of us here would. That is my point. We'd be the only ones aware she is playing this role."

Rex heard the logic in Dora's answer, but chose to ignore it. "I still don't like it. As you well know, the slope into a lifetime of danger is slippery. Why put her on it at all?"

"Your sister is one of the most focused and levelheaded individuals I've ever met," Dora said. "She takes after your grandmother. Caledonia will not look fondly on you making decisions for her. I say we tell her, and let her choose."

Frustration burned the back of Rex's throat. The worst of it was that Dora spoke rightly. His grandmother's intractability was one of her best qualities. He wanted his sister to know her own mind. Determination and self-confidence made for a coat of armour against the proverbial daggers of high society.

There was no point in fighting the battle here with Dora. He'd make sure Caledonia considered Audley's request with eyes wide open.

Lord Audley rested his hands upon his knees and levelled his gaze on Rex. "I do not make this request lightly. That said, Caledonia has full right of refusal. In time, I can find someone else. My fear is that I will be too late. I am operating in the dark as to the significance of the timing of the letter I received."

Rex took the envelopes from Dora and tucked them into the inner pocket of his jacket. "We will discuss this with Caledonia and get back with her decision."

Lord Audley inclined his head in acknowledgement, revealing the new strands of white in his hair. "Your promises to help bring me great comfort already. You have my permission to speak with Inga and Harris as well. Harris's training as a detective will be of great use."

Rex and Dora took their leave, exiting the house the same way they arrived. On the return trip, Rex took no joy from the underground journey.

Travelling deep beneath the surface reminded him too much of a grave.

Chapter 3
A Case Like No Other

D ora spent the journey home planning their next steps. She had already decided to treat this like any other assignment. Each case brought its own unique set of challenges, and this one was no different.

Lost in thought as she was, she failed to notice that Rex wasn't keeping up. She slowed her steps to wait for him. He, too, had much weighing on his mind.

"Dearest, would you mind terribly if we spoke to Inga and Harris before we contact Callie?" he asked.

"Because you are holding out hope they will agree with your desire to keep her out of it?"

"In vain, but yes. Can you blame me?"

Dora couldn't argue with that remark. She'd learned the hard way about the folly of keeping her brother at arm's length. Rex could try to keep Caledonia at a distance, but she had little faith he would do any better. Unfortunately, some lessons had to be learned firsthand.

They followed an alley between two buildings until they reached the back gate to their Belgravia home. Once inside, they pulled the wigs from their heads and shook their hair loose.

Dora pulled the pins free from hers and tucked them into her pocket.

"Yoo hoo?" she called from the kitchen door. The cook glanced up and expressed no surprise at finding her mistress dressed like a housemaid on her half-day off. "Are Harris and Inga at home?"

The cook stopped stirring a pot long enough to point upstairs. Dora swiped a fresh bun from a cooling tray on her way past. When Rex tried to repeat the trick, the rosy-cheeked cook swatted him away.

"It is bad enough Miss Dora acts with such disregard, but given everything else she does, I've abandoned all hope of refining her. You, on the other hand, my lord," Cook said, returning to her pot, "are a paragon in comparison. Fear not, though. I'll send one of the twins up with a tea tray. Get changed, and you can have as many as you like."

Dora took pity on her husband and divided her spoils in half. The rich flavour of currants, sugar, and butter did little to satiate her hunger after their trek across town. Thus incentivised, they made quick work of getting back into their normal wardrobe.

Inga and Harris sat in the drawing room, arguing over which moving picture show to see at the weekend. Dora clapped her hands to get their attention.

"Good news, my friends. Our days of being layabouts are at an end once again. Lord Audley needs our full attention on a personal matter."

Inga poured tea for everyone. "We guessed as much last night. I take it you got the rest of the story?"

"Indeed. This is a twisty tale, so pay attention." Dora recounted the story. At the right moment, Rex produced the letters. He echoed Audley's request to keep them in order. Inga and Harris took the top two envelopes from the stack and perused the contents. They held the letters side-by-side, but that didn't make them comprehensible.

"Are these written using the same cipher?" Harris asked.

"We don't know," Dora answered honestly. Her gaze drifted to Rex, waiting for him to speak up. He remained stubbornly silent. "Audley wants us to ask Caledonia to try her hand at deciphering them. What do you two think of the suggestion?"

Harris frowned. "Really? But she is so young and inexperienced."

"She is also a safe choice," Inga reminded her husband.

Dora wasn't surprised in the least by Inga's ability to put herself in Lord Audley's shoes. It was this skill that made Inga so useful during Dora's spy missions. Lord Audley was rarely there in person. Dora had the next best thing.

"I take it His Grace had no other cryptologists available."

"It would seem not. He was remarkably closed-mouth when I broached the topic. Which brings us nicely back to Caledonia. Do we ask for her help or not?"

Harris grimaced again, but kept quiet. He was wise enough to see the writing on the wall. Rex gave Inga a hopeful glance, but she shook her head.

"Your sister would be most cross if she discovered you excluded her. Do yourselves both a favour and ask." Inga waved Rex on. "Ring her now. We'll wait."

The house telephone sat on a table near the front entry. The group held their tongues so they could listen to Rex's half of the conversation. The brief call gave them little to work with. Rex returned a moment later.

"She was at loose ends, so she said she'd come right over."

"Do you want me to send Archie to collect her?" Harris asked.

Rex brushed aside the offer. "She said she'd have Grandmama's driver bring her around."

Rex settled back beside Dora. His erect posture and tight shoulders betrayed his discomfort at how this day was progressing. While Dora sought for the words to reassure him, Harris spoke up and made things worse.

"I hate to be the killjoy, but even if Caledonia agrees to help, I fear you will still be in over your heads. Decrypting the letters is the least of your problems. This case is icy cold. If Lord Audley couldn't solve it, and he was there at the time, how will we do it now?"

Dora gritted her teeth. It was a fair question. Still, she wasn't ready to admit defeat before they started. "Until a month or so ago, Lord Audley wasn't aware this problem existed. Almost as soon as it crossed his desk, he handed it off. The only thing he has put his mind toward is getting someone else to handle this."

"You can hardly blame him," Inga added. "For us, this is a cold case. For him, it is a minefield of emotions threatening to explode at the first misstep."

Harris shook his head. "I hear what you are saying, but it doesn't change the fact that we are not investigators. Or, not in the traditional sense."

"You are," Dora pointed out.

"I am one man. Cases of this nature require multiple, disparate lines of investigation. There will be research involved, reticent witnesses to track down and cajole, and other brick walls built by the passage of time."

Dora could hardly believe her ears. Had Harris lost faith in their abilities? Debate was always welcome, but this went well beyond that line.

Dora searched the faces of Inga and Rex, expecting one of them to voice her thoughts. Instead, they bore the same pensive expression as Harris. Why?

Dora bit back a hot-headed retort. Harris had never stood in opposition to any of her plans. During his days on the police force, he'd been a damned talented investigator. Good enough, even, to challenge Dora and win Inga's heart. Only a fool would ignore him.

Dora was no fool.

In a carefully modulated tone, she began again. "Lord Audley has dedicated his life to this great nation. This is the first time I've known him to ask anything in return. I hear your concerns, but I must ask you to view them in a new light. We cannot say no to his request. Therefore, what do we need in order to say yes?"

Harris wiped a hand across his face. He stared off into the distance, gathering his thoughts. "The first thing we'll need is time. We can't go into this mystery expecting it to run like our other cases. If we are to do this, you must manage Lord Audley's expectations."

"I can do that," Dora promised.

"Second, we need more manpower."

If Harris expected that to give Dora pause, he was in for disappointment. His words provided an open door. Dora turned her head to check whether Rex's mind was travelling in the same direction. He met her gaze with an impish smile.

"This is exactly the sort of opportunity we needed," Rex said.

"Opportunity?" Harris asked.

"To bring Clark into the fold," Inga answered. "That is what you mean to do."

"Yes, but only with Lord Audley's permission." Dora's smile widened. "We couldn't have asked for a better proving ground. We don't even need to reveal all. Clark won't question why we're helping Lord Audley with a private matter. Furthermore, Clark owes Lord Audley for keeping him safe during our investigation at Windsor Castle. We can position it as a chance to return a favour!"

"Don't get ahead of yourself," Inga cautioned. "First, let's ask Lord Audley. Since I know patience is not one of your virtues, I suggest we send Archie around with a note. Despite his brawny build, he is excellent at passing unnoticed."

The trill of the doorbell interrupted the conversation. Harris leapt to his feet to go answer it. A moment later, Dora heard him welcome Caledonia inside. He showed her to the drawing room and then left to make arrangements with Archie.

Caledonia rushed over to embrace Dora, Rex, and then Inga in turn. Her youthful exuberance blew through the drawing room like a gust of fresh air. The doubts and concerns of the earlier conversation swept clear, leaving a blank slate for their next chat.

Dora studied her sister-in-law. The time in Rome had worked wonders on the young woman's confidence. It wasn't just because she'd studied under a world-renowned maestro. Dora had trusted Caledonia with the secret of her heritage. Bearing the weight of that information had aided in her maturity.

Now back in London, Caledonia was further stretching her wings. She'd adopted Louise Brook's style, wearing her pale blonde hair in a bold shingle. The short style flattered her sharp cheekbones and long neck. Despite the fashionable cut and modern, drop-waisted frock, Caledonia wasn't the sort to trade on her looks. She engaged deeply in discussions related to her areas of interest. Hiding her prodigious intellect was the furthest thing from her mind.

Dora loved her for that.

The two women, now family by marriage, had needed no time to find common ground. That ground was about to expand.

"My mind is awhirl, wondering why you'd want to see me. I have a lengthy list of guesses, but perhaps it is faster for you to tell me." Caledonia blinked innocently at her brother. "What is going on?"

Dora sat back in her chair, ceding the floor to Rex. Rather than answering Caledonia, Rex replied with a question. "Did you enjoy deciphering those old letters?"

Caledonia's brow wrinkled. "Huh? You made me rush across town to ask me that? Wait. Of course, you didn't. You have something - something in code."

Rex huffed. "Maybe, but first answer my question. Did you decrypt those letters out of boredom?"

Caledonia's face hardened as her enthusiasm took a back seat. "I have plenty to keep me busy, Rex. While my projects may not be as important to the rest of the world as yours, they are no less significant to me. Cryptography keeps my mind sharp and is fun as well."

Dora winced on Rex's behalf.

Rex held up his hands and launched into an apology. "I didn't mean to insult you, honest! I—but—"

"Might as well spit it out," Inga suggested in a gentle tone.

Rex ran his fingers through his hair, mucking up his oiled locks. "We have an opportunity for you to do more decryption, but it comes with risk."

Caledonia leaned forward. "You and Dora will keep me safe."

"From danger, yes. We'd do our best, regardless. But there is an additional risk. If you do this now, you may be asked again in the future. And by asked, I mean ordered. Even Grandmama might struggle to save you from duty."

"I see." Caledonia reclined back in her seat as the fire of her earlier indignation spluttered out. "That is not an outcome I foresaw. Truth be told, I don't have a ready answer."

"That is a wise response," Inga said. As the eldest in the room, she stepped in as the voice of reason. "The fact that you didn't say no straightaway is telling. Rex, if your sister is to decide, it must be with the full picture. Tell her what you need and then give her a night to sleep on it."

Rex picked up the pile of letters and offered them to his sister. "They belonged to Lady Audley. If you, or someone else, can tell us what they say, we mean to look into her death. It may not have been an accident."

Caledonia accepted the letters and tucked them into her handbag. "That is a very serious matter. Now I understand the implications. One last question before we move on to happier matters. Might I seek guidance from Grandmama?"

Rex looked at Dora. She gave a single nod.

"Grandmama will be an excellent sounding board." Rex sank back to rest against the sofa cushion. "You mentioned happier matters. Do you have news of your own?"

Caledonia sat up, with a smile lighting up her face. Her blue eyes glittered with excitement. "I do! I've been speaking with Grandmama, and she has agreed to support my application."

"Application?" Dora echoed. "For what?"

"For university. With any luck, soon I'll be a student at Oxford."

Chapter 4
Rex Goes Recruiting

P atrons crowded the American Bar at the Savoy, despite it
being midweek. The room was awash with the soft glow of
modern lamps, casting elegant patterns of light and shadow
across the polished mahogany and mirrored surfaces. A blend of
exotic fragrances mingled with the subtle aroma of fine spirits
and fresh citrus garnishes. The gentle clinking of crystal, low
hum of conversation, and the faint melodies of a piano playing
the latest jazz tunes set a rhythm that seemed to pulse through
the very heart of the room.

Behind the bar, the barman pushed up the sleeves of his
crisp, white jacket and took orders from the line of well-dressed
guests. He poured one libation after another into his cocktail
shaker before serving the requested drink.

It was those cocktails that gave the bar its name. The mixed
drinks had taken the world by storm. While Prohibition had
dried up glasses and capped the bottles on the other side of the
pond, here people were free to indulge. And indulge they did.

But not Rex and Dora. Or, at least not on this evening.
Despite their finery and wide smiles, they had business on their
minds. They paused inside the doorway to get their bearings.

"Why don't you make the rounds saying hello while I go order us glasses of champagne?" Rex proposed.

Dora straightened his black bowtie before sauntering off, her hips swaying beneath her satin gown with each step. The eyes of every red-blooded male in the room followed her progress.

At the bar, Rex ran into a familiar face. "Lord Benedict, what brings you here?"

Dora's brother waved to get the barman's attention. "Mother made me promise to squire one of her American relatives about town."

"Anyone I might have met?"

Benedict caught onto the subtext hidden in Rex's question. "I doubt it. I only met her myself this week. By the way, is Theodora here with you? My cousin is a fan of the society pages; she'd be thrilled to make the famous Miss Laurent's acquaintance."

"She is, indeed. I need to step out for a moment to handle a spot of business. You can keep her occupied while I'm away."

Benedict raised his eyebrows. "Is everything alright?"

"Right as rain. Theodora knows I've got to step out." Rex paused there, taking advantage of a passing waiter to order a glass of champagne. "Be a pal and take it to Theodora when it comes. I'll be back before she's had time to miss me."

Benedict promised to keep an eye on her, for all that would do. Should Dora decide to get up to no good, Benedict didn't have a hope of stopping her.

Rex ducked out through a side door into the staff area and followed a narrow corridor until he reached a door marked stairs. He took the steps two at a time until he was one floor up. There, he switched to the lift.

By now, he knew the way to the suite Lord Audley used for his clandestine meetings. The august peer waited in the sitting room, gazing out the window at the London skyline. He didn't turn around when Rex came in.

"Does Caledonia have an answer for me?" he asked.

"She does, but it comes with conditions."

Audley swung around. Backlit by the city lights, the white strands in his hair shone almost like a halo. But this man was no angel. The Dowager Duchess had advised her granddaughter accordingly.

"She'll do it?"

"Yes. Believe me, that was the easy part. The rest of what I'm about to say comes directly from my grandmother."

Lord Audley settled into a cushioned chair and motioned for Rex to join him.

Rex chose the leather armchair on the other side of the low table, facing his mentor head on. He crossed his leg over his knee and relaxed, wanting to appear in control. When he had Lord Audley's undivided attention, he explained, "Caledonia has expressed her intentions to study at university."

"I respect her choice."

"Respect isn't enough," Rex said. "You must agree to do nothing to stand in her way. Should this assignment of ours drag on, you will release her when it is time for her to depart. Grandmother is most insistent on this matter."

"Tell her - tell them both - they have nothing to fear. While I may have a reputation for ruthlessness, I have never forced anyone to work for me. That is a commitment that must be freely given, as you experienced."

"I do. That is the only reason my grandmother didn't stand in Caledonia's way."

At that remark, Lord Audley barked a laugh. "May I add a codicil to this gentlemen's agreement?"

Rex's eyebrows shot up.

"Before Caledonia submits her applications for a place, I'd

like the chance to offer her some advice of my own. The world is changing. Universities are finally awarding degrees to women. Soon, other organisations will grow wise to the talents of the fairer sex. With Caledonia's unique set of skills, there will be opportunities of which she isn't aware. I'd like to tell her about them."

Rex could not find a reason to deny the man's request. His grandmother would most certainly embrace it. Rex offered Lord Audley his hand. "We have a deal. Let's shake on it like gentlemen, so we can move on to my next order of business."

Audley gripped Rex's hand and shook it. There was no hint of his age in the forceful hold. Despite the salt in his pepper hair, the man was still in his prime.

Rex pulled his hand back and rested it on his leg. "Let us speak now about Lord Clark."

Audley's shoulders tensed.

Rex lifted his hand to stop Audley there. "You need not raise your objections, as I can well imagine them. Instead, I'd like to give you a reason to say yes - one you might not have considered."

Audley shifted position in his chair and raised one hand to his chin. "Go on, then. I'm listening."

"Have you considered training a successor?"

"A what?" Lord Audley spluttered.

Rex was expecting such a reaction. He carried on. "You say the world is changing, yet much remains the same. Someone is always vying for power. They will do whatever it takes to get it. Although I hope we never see another war like this last one, I'm not fool enough to believe it is impossible. The trip to Rome opened my eyes. Italy was our ally, a winner, and yet they seethe at the mere mention of the war. One day, they may seek to gain that which they believe they are owed."

"You speak truth, Rex, but what has that to do with Lord Clark?"

"You won't be here forever. None of us will. Listening to Caledonia talk about her dreams made me think about what comes next. Who in England will fill your shoes? They must be immune to the political jostling, wealthy enough to turn down bribes, dedicated to right, and wise enough to recognise what right is.

"Even if I aspired to the role, I cannot do what I do now *and* be known as your protégé. When I survey the field of men my age who show these qualities, I am left with few, if any at all. Clark is the closest you can come. He lacks wisdom and experience, but he has courage and conviction. With your tutelage, he will grow into a force for the good of this nation."

Rex stopped there, tamping the desire to list more arguments. Audley was not stupid.

The older man did not rush to respond. Rex counted that as a point in his favour. Audley's eyes widened and then narrowed again as he contemplated the matter.

Rex drew in a breath when his mentor straightened up. He braced himself for the man's reply. It was ingrained in his nature to accept the decision of those higher in rank. But Dora had taught him the importance of standing up for his beliefs.

"If it were anyone else making these statements, I'd laugh them out of the room. You are not one for pranks. Do you truly believe Lord Clark is worthy of such a post?"

Rex gave a single nod. "He will rise to the occasion. He always has. Few have given him the chance."

"I make no promises other than to give him a fair shake. You may recruit him for this assignment, but nothing more. If he impresses me, as you say he will, we can peel back another layer of this onion."

Rex kept his composure, despite the warm glow of

satisfaction coursing through his veins. He rose from his chair, said his goodbyes, and left before his smile broke free to give him away.

Downstairs in the American Bar, Rex found Dora sitting hip to hip at a corner table with Clark himself. The man was in jovial spirits, recounting their misadventures to Benedict and his American cousin.

Rex clapped him on the back and said hello. He did not take Clark up on the offer of his seat. "We're due at our next engagement soon, don't you recall?"

Clark's gaze clouded in confusion. To the man's credit, he played along. "I'd lost track of the time, old chap. We should get on our way. It was a pleasure to meet you, Miss Carnegie."

Without a backward glance, Rex, Clark, and Dora beelined for the door. A valet brought round Rex's Rolls-Royce. Clark slid into the back seat and waited until they'd pulled out onto the Strand before voicing his confusion.

"I'm not one to turn down an invitation, but where are we going? It was sheer happenstance that I ran into Theodora in the Savoy."

"It wasn't chance, but fate. We're in need of your help with a matter."

Clark shook off his air of insouciance. "Colour me intrigued. Where are we going?"

Rex glanced at Dora, letting his eyes communicate that all was well with Lord Audley. "To Theodora's, if that is acceptable to you both."

Rex made good time driving through the centre of London. He decided to credit Madame Fate with that, as well. It boded well for their investigation to believe the universe was on their side.

Harris showed them in and took their coats and hats. Dora poured glasses of wine while they waited for Inga and Harris to join them. In short order, the sleuthing team assembled once again.

Rex began. "Clark, as you are aware, we've done a favour or two for Lord Audley in the past. He has approached me again. This time, however, the request is personal. I will not ask you to hold your tongue on this matter because you'll do so in any case. But before I draw you behind the curtains, as it is, I'll give you the chance to say yes or no. Do you still wish to help us? To help Lord Audley?"

Clark sobered. "For the man to ask for assistance, it must be a serious matter. You may count upon me and my discretion."

"Excellent. There is one other thing you should know. Harris, here, has not always been a butler, nor did he rise through the traditional ranks. He was a detective, now retired."

"That explains his choice of cummerbunds and vests," Clark muttered, earning a laugh.

"I daresay no other mistress of the house would allow such leeway. I fell in love with Inga, but she refused to leave Theodora on her own. This disguise, if you will, seemed a reasonable solution."

"A hundred questions come to mind, but I'll table them until we've resolved our current matter." Clark turned his attention back to Rex. "What does Lord Audley need from us?"

"He wants us to find out whether someone murdered his wife."

Clark jerked backwards, causing his wine to slosh onto his hand. He dug through his coat pocket for a handkerchief and then asked Rex to explain what he meant. "Audley's wife died years ago, unless he married again with no one finding out... And at the rate this evening is going, I'm half-afraid you will say the latter is correct."

Dora chuckled. "No, there has been only one Lady Audley in his time. His longtime mistress has placed no such demands."

Clark eyed his glass and set it on a nearby table. He steepled his fingers across his chest. "Then you are going to have to explain. Was she, or was she not murdered? Is that our only question, or does he expect us to identify her possible killer? And why now?"

Rex replied, "I will tell you everything we know, although it is blessed little at this point. This will not be a simple case, if any of ours have ever been. But we have triumphed in the past, under equally difficult circumstances, so do not count us out before we begin."

It took the better part of an hour to bring Clark up to speed. He asked questions throughout, some smart and some not so much. Rex answered them all as best he could.

Dora had taught him that there was no harm in asking anything. Better he look like a fool in private than risk misunderstanding or making a careless mistake. He offered Clark that same latitude.

For his part, Clark took it all in stride. Even the news that Caledonia would act as a code-breaker barely gave him pause. "When your sister talks about music, I'm lucky to understand every third word. Her intelligence has never been in doubt."

Finally, the discussions wound down. The hour was late, and they had a long day in front of them.

Clark stood. "When do we start?"

"Tomorrow, at three in the afternoon, at Lord Audley's. He is going to tell us about his wife."

Chapter 5
The Mysterious Lady Audley

D ora often visited Lord Audley's home for a briefing. He'd provide her with dossiers and flag relevant press articles. She'd file the information away in her prodigious memory. While there, she'd make a sarcastic remark. He'd take her down a notch or two. Above all, they shared a feeling of camaraderie. They were secret soldiers fighting in the same war.

That was about to change.

Dora had made a point never to pry into her mentor's personal life. He returned the favour. But to solve this case, she'd have to cross that line. It hardly mattered that he invited her to do so.

Although Dora kept a smile on her face during the drive across town, inside, she feared her relationship with her mentor was about to undergo a fundamental change. It remained to be seen whether this turned out to be good or bad.

Basil, Dora's other footman, chauffeured Dora and Rex to Lord Audley's doorstep. The drive saw them past the private homes of Belgravia as they gave way to the bustling thoroughfares lined with luxury boutiques and galleries.

Gentlemen in tailored suits and ladies in the latest fashions from Paris promenaded along the pavements, while street vendors and newsboys added a lively hum to the scene. Soon enough, the lush expanse of Hyde Park offered a verdant respite amidst the urban landscape, with horse-drawn carriages and the occasional automobile passing by.

Like much of the upperclass, the duke had a spacious mansion in Mayfair, a stone's throw from Grosvenor Square. Constructed from pristine Portland stone, the building's exterior glowed softly under the London sun. The entrance, framed by a pair of Corinthian columns, supported an ornate pediment. Above, evenly spaced sash windows lined the stone facade, each adorned with intricate ironwork balconies. The residence sat discreetly back from the square, its dignity preserved by a low stone wall and a small landscaped forecourt. That buffer from the urban energy of London's busy streets suggested a realm where time-honoured elegance and tranquillity reigned supreme.

Yet, the occupants in the car were well aware that appearances could often be deceiving. Rex reached for the door handle but stopped short of opening the door. He gazed at the exterior with a conflicted expression on his face. "Seems strange, doesn't it?"

"Entering through the front door?" Dora asked, pointing at the glossy black painted entrance.

"Well, yes. That, too. I meant coming here to question Audley."

Dora scooted closer and kissed Rex on the cheek. In the front seat, Basil kept his gaze facing forward.

"What was that for?" Rex asked.

"For reading my mind. You'd best get out now as I see Clark walking down the street."

Clark's wobbly smile turned to one filled with relief when Rex hailed him. For a man who'd faced much, including battle against a murderous enemy, the prospect of prying into Lord Audley's past had left him a bundle of nerves.

Dora flashed her pearly whites at him. "My advice is to treat him like any other caged beast."

Clark twisted the edge of his moustache. "With trepidation and never turning my back?"

Rex clapped Clark on the arm. "Only if you want him to eat you alive. You aren't encroaching on his territory. He's invited us in. Treat him with the same respect you'd give any other peer, and all will be fine."

"That's peer with a lowercase p,'" Dora clarified.

Clark shook off his nerves, and they climbed the front steps to ring the bell. Lord Audley awaited them in his private study. He had eschewed his desk chair in favour of a simple, velvet-upholstered wingback near the fireplace. He arose and invited them to join him.

Dora, Rex, and Clark arranged themselves in the remaining chairs. As soon as they sat, he began. "I suspect this is no easier for you than me. The good news is that a quarter of a century ago, I had far fewer secrets. Please ask anything. My natural reticence will do us no good."

"Understood," Rex said. Clark echoed his reply.

Dora gave Lord Audley an audacious wink. Her cheeky response broke the tension in the room. Audley relaxed into his chair and took a deep breath.

"I will start at the beginning of my relationship with Daphne. I married later than many of my peers. I thought it a wise choice to bide my time. While they danced around the ballrooms and paid calls on each season's debutantes, I was free to accumulate power. It took me some time to understand that marriage was another way to achieve my goals."

"No tales of scandalous ankle glimpses and contrived meetings in moonlit gardens, I take it?" Dora asked.

"None that are relevant to this, Miss Laurent," Audley replied. But he smiled nonetheless, and Dora counted that as a win.

"Daphne was the daughter of Lord and Lady Arrington — a fine family with a distinguished lineage. She shared my view on what made for a good match. I spoke with Lord Arrington, and he gave his blessing. We married six months later." He stopped, his gaze slipping off to the side, lost in thought. "We were happy with one another. I admired her strength of character. I'd like to think Daphne felt the same."

Rex broke in with a question. "Now that you are looking back, does hindsight change your view of your relationship?"

"Until I found the coded letters in her things, I never doubted where I stood with her. It is impossible to look at them and not wonder if I was a great fool."

"Tell us about your wife. Did she have any hobbies? Who were her friends?" Dora asked.

"Much the same as any other lady of her generation. She attended society events, hosted charity luncheons, and embroidered in her spare time."

"No secret vices?" Dora teased. "No one is perfect."

Audley grimaced. "Daphne's only weakness was her stallion, Merlin. She'd spend hours in the stables, brushing his coat and feeding him carrots. Merlin returned the affection by ferrying her wherever she wished to go. I never understood how she could have died. The stable master said such things happen. Maybe a bee stung the horse, or it stepped wrong. Whatever happened must have caught her off guard and she tumbled off. It was an unfortunate accident... or not."

Dora's gaze slid over to meet Rex's. He, too, heard the pain in Audley's voice.

Clark kept them on track. "Is it possible your wife had another reason to go riding?"

"If you are suggesting she had an affair, do not fear saying the words. As you can imagine, it was the first thing to cross my mind."

Dora sat up. "You hired the private investigator to look into that aspect. Given we are all here, I assume he came up dry. However, it would be useful to know what he did and with whom he spoke. There is little point in us retreading the same ground if the man was as capable as you say."

Lord Audley rose and went to his desk. He retrieved two large envelopes. The first, he passed to Dora. "This is his report. He spoke with each of her friends and her lady's maid."

"What excuse did he offer?" Rex asked. "Surely he didn't come right out and suggest Lady Audley was murdered."

"Indeed, he did not. He told them he was working on a divorce case on behalf of a society wife. The woman claimed her husband had a long history of infidelity. He was to gather the evidence."

"And that worked?" Clark was agog.

"Well enough for the chap to get past the butlers. Mind you, I doubt it would work in reverse. Women want to help other women, especially in such a serious matter." Audley shrugged his shoulders. "He pressed them on whether it was possible Daphne had been seeing someone. To a one, they all said no. They were emphatic she had always been loyal. She was not the type to lose her head and betray me. Especially not with a married man," he added.

A question sprang to Dora's mind. "When the investigator spoke to her maid, did he ask her about the letters you found?"

"He did not because he did not know of their existence. I trust you understand why I kept that information close to my vest." Audley handed the second envelope to Rex. "That brings us nicely to your investigation. Inside, you will find my shortlist of enemies and rivals from that time in my life."

Audley waited while Rex opened the envelope and skimmed the single typed page. Rex's face did not betray his thoughts. Dora held out her hand, but he failed to pass it over.

Rex tucked it in his jacket pocket. "We will look into each of these men, but it would be most helpful to understand what matters held your focus back then."

"It was the summer of 1898. Britain remained focused on Hong Kong, where we were negotiating the ninety-nine-year extension of our grant of ownership. My top priority was securing our East-West trading rights."

Rex arched an eyebrow. "These men opposed you on that matter?"

"Not necessarily. There was another world issue weighing on Europe."

"The Spanish-American war," Clark said, surprising everyone, himself included. "I can't believe I remembered that."

"Next time, keep that last part to yourself," Rex suggested, causing Clark to flush.

Lord Audley ignored their banter. "The war between Spain and America was completely unnecessary. All the European powers lobbied for common sense to gain the upper hand, but the American press had the country's population inflamed with indignation."

For once, Dora's memory came up short. She recollected that there had been a war, and that the United States had gained valuable territory as a result. But Britain's involvement escaped her. She stopped short of chastising herself. A brief skirmish, long settled, hadn't warranted her attention until now.

She decided to remedy her failing immediately. Clark still thought her a foreigner. This was to her advantage. She thickened her French accent before asking, "I am not familiar with this war. Would you mind telling me more about it?"

"Ostensibly, they went to war over control of Cuba. Several years of insurgence and crackdowns between the Spanish and the locals had resulted in terrible suffering. The US swooped in to save the Cubans... Or so they claimed. In February of that year, a US ship, positioned near Havana, suffered an explosion and sank, taking most of its crew with her. The American government insisted Spain was responsible, and would hear no arguments to the contrary."

"Were the Spanish to blame?" Rex asked.

Lord Audley threw up his hands. "The Americans said yes, the Spanish said no. In the end, the real identity of the culprit was irrelevant. The tide of public sentiment demanded satisfaction for the dead, and independence for the Cubans. The US navy far outclassed that of the Spaniards. They swiftly defeated them. The implications, however, were much farther reaching. The Spaniards ceded control of Puerto Rico and the Philippines, on top of leaving Cuba. By January 1899, the US ranked officially as a world power."

Dora did not need overlong to contemplate the ramifications of Audley's words. Such a rapid loss would not have happened without the rest of Europe staying clear of the fight. To make that happen, the Americans would have dispatched people like her to all the major cities, London included. They'd have looked for friends to argue their case.

Friends like Dora's father, the Duke of Dorset.

Married to an American, in a love match no less, Lord Cavendish would have been a friendly ear for his wife's countrymen.

Lord Audley had put her father's name on his list. It shouldn't have come as a surprise, especially given their long history of standing opposite one another. Still, it rankled that Audley thought her father capable of murdering his wife.

That was why Rex had pocketed Audley's list. He hoped to spare her the matter. That was the coward's way out. Although acid burned the back of her throat, she firmed her resolve. She'd begun her day worried for Lord Audley. He wasn't the only one facing a test. If he could open the lid on his past, she could do no less than face into her fears in the present.

Chapter 6
Clark Takes a Ride

Rex found himself in a conundrum. He had been from the moment he laid eyes on Lord Audley's suspect list. If he'd put any forethought into the matter, he'd have expected to see certain names.

But Dora's father?

Seeing Lord Cavendish's title typed in such precise letters had made his stomach roil. He'd folded the paper and tucked it away, as much to protect Dora as himself.

His instincts screamed that Dora's father couldn't be a murderer. Surely, Lord Audley must have by now learned that the man had lines he wouldn't dare to cross. Yet, he'd added his arch rival's name to the list and passed it over, knowing it would land like a cannon ball, punching a hole through their resolve and willingness to help.

Rex followed Dora and Clark through the house and back onto the pavement. He heard Dora tell Clark to meet at her house and caught Clark's confirmation of the plan. But he didn't dare open his mouth, unsure what to say.

Dora caught him by the lapels and forced him to meet her gaze head on. "You don't need to hide it from me."

Rex's eyes widened, and he shook his head.

"My father's name was on the list. It seems impossible he could be to blame for a death, but we must work through the investigation all the same. I firmly believe our thoroughness will clear his name. Do you agree?"

Rex swallowed and blinked to clear his gaze. Dora stared up at him with such an earnest expression on her face. It grounded him better than anything anyone else might have said. As his fears eased, the words flowed. "Whatever we find, we do so together. You will not deal with this alone."

Dora raised a hand and cupped his cheek. "I can always count upon you... and Inga, Harris, Archie, Cynthia, and Basil — who is waiting in the car. We'd better hurry. Clark is going to beat us there."

Indeed, they arrived home to find Clark standing in her drawing room, with Mews winding between his legs while he updated Inga and Harris on all that Lord Audley had said.

"Sit, all of you," Dora instructed. She rang for tea and took her place beside Rex on the sofa.

"That's quite some tale," Harris said, after everyone had a fresh cup of tea. "In one circumstance, Lady Audley died at the hands of her lover. In another, someone used her as a pawn in a political game. Which one do you feel is most likely?"

"The former," Rex said without hesitation. "Lord Audley must feel the same, given he hired an investigator to look into the possibility. Thus far, however, nothing has come to light."

"So, she didn't have an affair?" Clark asked.

"Not necessarily," Harris intervened. "Often, getting the truth hinges on asking the right person the right question. I'm impressed by the investigator's approach when speaking with Lady Audley's friends, but he overlooked an inherent weakness. Women protect women, especially their dearest friends. Take Inga and Theodora. They'd lie straight to my face if the situation required. The investigator asked Lady Audley's friends to share her darkest secrets to help some nebulous unidentified woman. It is also possible they told the truth, and Lady Audley wasn't sleeping with a married man. That still leaves open the chance she had an affair with someone unattached."

"I hadn't thought of that," Clark admitted. "We've barely begun and already I am out of my depths. How will I be of any use?"

"Even the most seasoned detective is out of his depths at the start of a case. Think of how we approached the murder investigation in Rome. We asked many questions, turned over stones, and examined what lay underneath. We will do so again," Harris replied. "Which brings us neatly to our next steps. Where do you want to go next?"

Rex weighed the options. "We've got three pathways to explore. The first is the possibility of an affair. The second is the list of Audley's enemies. Last, but not least, is the question of who sent Lord Audley the message that started all of this off."

"All are of equal importance," Dora said. "I say we split up. Rex and Clark, why don't you take Audley's list? You two definitely have more familiarity with the men on there than I do.

Rex struggled to keep a straight face at Dora's bald-faced lie. It was as if she'd wanted to prove her earlier point to those in the know, anyway. That didn't make her recommendation any less valid. If they were to keep an open mind regarding her father, she'd need to keep her distance at the start.

Rex retrieved the list from his pocket and laid it on the table. "There are three names — Lord Cavendish, Lord Stanley, and Sir Geoffrey. All were and still are active in the House of Lords."

"Then we should go there," Clark said. "There are extensive records of committee meetings. We could check the month leading up to Lady Audley's death. If someone was making a move, we'll see hints of it in the meeting minutes."

"If nothing else, it will give us a place to start with our questions," Rex said. "We can hardly approach men at that level with a fishing expedition. They will make sure that we are expelled without hesitation."

"That's assuming we can get a meeting with them in the first place," Clark reminded him. "Theodora, how will you handle Lady's Audley's friends? Are you acquainted with any of them?"

Dora took the private detective's folder of notes and flipped to the relevant page. She skipped past the names of the ladies interviewed. She had something different in mind. "Harris, would you mind fetching Cook?"

Harris's gaze narrowed as he eyed her with suspicion. "Is our cook somehow involved?"

"I should hope not," Dora answered in a bland tone. "She makes a most excellent Beef Wellington, and I'd hate to have to let her go. All will become clear if you ask her to come here."

A few minutes later, Dora's cook followed Harris into the room. She was a middle-aged woman with brown hair showing the first hints of grey. She wiped her hands upon her apron and lifted her head into a proud pose.

"What can I do for you, Miss Theodora?"

"Are you familiar with anyone residing in the Wilson household?" she asked, naming the household where Lady Audley's maid now worked.

"Their cook, of course. I often bump into her at the market. Lovely woman, I must say."

"Excellent!" Dora's smile widened. "I need her to deliver a

message. I'd like to have a word with Lady Wilson's maid. Her name is Penny Brown."

"Is she in some kind of trouble?"

"No, not at all. We need her help with a matter of some importance. Inga and I can meet her at her convenience. Perhaps there is a cafe nearby, somewhere close enough that she could step out for an hour without being missed?"

"Leave it with me, miss. I'll have a place and time for you before supper is on the table."

After Cook left, Clark asked, "Why are you starting with the lady's maid?"

"Two reasons," Dora replied. "First, she is most likely to know for a certainty if Lady Audley was stepping out. Second, she's also sitting atop my list of people who might have sent that note to Lord Audley."

Rex skimmed the faces of the people around him, checking whether there was anything else to be discussed. When no one spoke up, he set his teacup aside and suggested he and Clark take their leave. "No point in waiting until tomorrow to get started. In fact, it will likely be easier for us to search through the records at Westminster if most of the staff have already left for the day. No need then to offer any explanation."

"Good shout, old chap," Clark said. He and Rex gathered their coats and hats. Outside on the pavement, Clark checked his watch. "It's nearing five. The roads will be clogged."

Rex backed up a step and gave his friend a sly grin. "If you are up for an adventure, I know a surefire way to get across town without wasting time staring out our windows watching passersby."

Clark glanced down at his expensive leather shoes. "Please, don't suggest walking."

"Nothing of the sort," Rex said, clapping him on the back. "Have you ever ventured onto the underground?"

It took some convincing, but eventually Rex brought Clark around to the idea. "If nothing else, it is an excellent way to cover our tracks. We can chalk the whole day up to our usual sort of shenanigans. First the underground, then finding some obscure fact in the Parliament archives. No one will guess what we're really about."

"When you put it that way, how can I decline?" Clark checked his pocket for coins and then motioned for Rex to lead the way.

Clark reacted to London's famous underground like a kid in a candy store with money burning a hole in his pocket. His head swivelled left and right, his gaze jumping from the theatre bills posted on the walls to the street performer strumming a guitar. He uttered not a single word, so busy was he at taking it all in.

Even the smell of the underground, the world-weary Londoners slogging their way home, and the tightly packed carriages failed to dent his enthusiasm. When they arrived at Westminster Station, Clark sighed in disappointment that their journey was at an end.

"Why haven't I travelled this way before?" he asked, not expecting an answer. He spun around to look at Rex. "Not that I'm of the mind to abandon my Rolls, but I can see the benefit of slipping below ground now and again."

"Talk like that will have you revolutionising the lives of gentleman everywhere, Lord Clark," Rex quipped. "The gaps between social classes will close as England's peers stand shoulder-to-shoulder with clerks, tradesmen, lorry drivers, and bin men. Are you certain you are ready to instigate such a change?"

Although Rex meant his words as a jest, Clark took them seriously. The man stopped in his tracks, forcing those walking behind them to make a quick detour. Clark didn't hear a word of their complaints, despite the volume and vehemence with which they were issued. He was far too busy considering Rex's question.

Rex took him by the arm and moved him out of the middle of the pavement, guiding him to a space of blank wall between two shop fronts. From where they stood, Big Ben towered over the stately halls of Parliament. The air held the tang of salt water and smoke coming from the boats on the Thames.

The gulf between the classes was never more evident. On one side of Bridge Street, the leaders of the land issued the laws that governed them all. Where Rex and Clark stood, just outside Westminster Station, the common men and women hurried past, so immune to the sights that few spared a glance for London's most famous attraction.

Clark took it all in, his brow creased in deep thought. Finally, he spoke. "Maybe we should change, Rex. Our ivory towers offered no protection from war. Or death. Yet we wrap ourselves in soft furs and expensive leathers and pretend it won't happen to us again. But wars come and go. Even minor skirmishes like the one Audley referenced can cause profound changes."

"Indeed, they can," Rex agreed. He waited for Clark to say more, but the man grew quiet. That was all right. It sufficed for Rex to plant that seed of thought in his friend's mind. "We'd better get a move on if we want to have any hope of finishing before the dinner bell."

Clark launched into motion, stepping into a break in the pedestrian traffic. When they crossed the street and arrived at the main entrance to Westminster Palace, Clark groaned.

"What's the matter? Is something amiss?"

"Yes, indeed, there is." Clark covered his face with his hands and shook his head. "I've just realised we're to spend the rest of this lovely day locked in a room full of papers and no bottles of gin."

"Cheer up," Rex said, encouraging Clark with a smile. "Harris has been practicing his hand at making American cocktails. Find something useful, and I'm sure he'll mix you a drink as a reward."

Chapter 7
The First Letter

Cook came through with a meeting for the next day. Dora and Inga dressed appropriately for the outing, choosing innocuous dresses that would fit in at a simple cafe. They left the men of the house hard at work.

Clark had turned up after breakfast, looking surprisingly dapper despite the early hour. He, Rex, and Harris had rolled up their sleeves. The men had boxes of papers to sort through, borrowed from the Parliament archives office with the express agreement to return them within two days.

Dora half-expected Clark to beg off or to offer to accompany her, but he was taking his assignment seriously. He had produced a pair of reading glasses she had never seen and perched them on his nose. One after another, he flipped through the pages of each box, his brow scrunched in concentration. He had not even commented when Mews leapt onto the table and demanded attention with a plaintive miaow. He had, however, drawn a line when the cat batted a scrap of paper from his hand.

Dora and Inga held their laughter in until they exited the house. Despite the overcast sky, the women had a sunny outlook. Progress, even slow, was something to celebrate.

Lady Audley's former maid now worked for the wife of a parliamentary minister. As the family also lived in Belgravia, Dora and Inga chose to walk.

"Do you still plan to be honest with Miss Collins?" Inga asked while they waited to cross a street.

"Can you see any upside to opting for subterfuge?" Dora replied. When Inga failed to reply, she glanced at her. "Then why pose the question?"

Inga cast Dora a withering glance. "Because subterfuge is your middle name."

"In point of fact, my middle name is Jane, just like Miss Collins."

"A fine English name it is," Inga replied. "But I can't imagine you plan to share that fact with our companion."

"Touché," Dora said, shrugging her shoulders in defeat. "I walked right into that, didn't I?"

Inga threw out her arm to keep Dora from walking in front of a passing cyclist. "Do us both a favour and open your eyes— and I mean that figuratively and literally."

The meeting point was a narrow cafe tucked into a side street. Dora immediately grasped the reason behind Miss Collins' choice. The clean front window and carefully swept doorway spoke to the pride of the owner. The narrow shape meant someone sitting in the back would not be visible from the road.

Miss Collins wanted to keep their meeting private. Dora and Inga agreed. They entered the building. A small bell above the door trilled in response, announcing the arrival of more customers.

Inside, worn wooden tables and mismatched chairs offered a simple setting, while the lingering scent of strong tea and the comforting warmth of freshly toasted bread filled the air. The soft murmur of chatter among the working-class patrons created a cosy atmosphere.

An older woman stood behind a counter decorated with plates of iced buns, fresh scones, and biscuits. Dora's eye was drawn to the golden layers of a Victoria Sponge. One glance and she could taste the tart sweetness of the berry jam in the middle.

Inga's gaze shifted in a different direction. She nudged Dora's arm and tilted her head, motioning toward the woman sitting alone at the far end of the room.

There were numerous reasons to believe the woman to be Miss Collins. The grey strands in her dark hair, pulled tight in a neat bun, and lines bracketing her eyes proclaimed her to be the right age. The neat black dress was easily identifiable as a maid's uniform.

Furthermore, although alone, she sat at a table with three chairs.

Dora and Inga walked past the other occupied tables until they reached the woman's side.

"Miss Collins?" Dora asked. When the woman nodded, they sat in the remaining chairs. The proprietress bustled over to take their orders. Dora requested tea and a generous slice of cake, despite the morning hour. Inga limited herself to a hot drink. With Dora's encouragement, Miss Collins ordered tea and toasted crumpets.

They completed the introductions while they waited for their food. Inga went first, followed by Dora. For once, Dora didn't go with one of her lesser-used pseudonyms. She introduced herself as Miss Laurent.

Miss Collins's eyes widened into saucers. "I thought your face was familiar. My mistress is an avid reader of the society pages."

They paused there to distribute the tray of drinks and food among themselves. Dora poured milk into the teas and offered spoonfuls of sugar. Miss Collins hardly knew how to respond to someone of the upper class treating her as an honoured guest.

Dora's efforts weren't for naught. When they got down to business, they found Miss Collins to be most accommodating. "The note indicated that you had inquiries regarding a former employer of mine."

"Yes, but before we get into them, allow me to explain why we're here. As you may know, my beau Lord Rex is somewhat of a protégé of Lord Audley. His Grace received a disturbing message some weeks back that suggested Lady Audley's death was no accident."

"Is that why that detective visited me?" Miss Collins asked.

"Yes. The detective was working for His Grace but was unable to learn anything new. I believe it was because circumstances required him to keep the reason for the investigation a secret. When Lord Audley shared the findings, or should I say lack thereof, Rex and I offered to take a different approach. That's why Miss Kay and I are here."

"I see." Miss Collins took a sip of her tea. Her eyes flicked from left to right. "I'm not sure how much help I can be. It isn't proper for a lady's maid to violate her mistress's trust, even if she is no longer living. I'm not the type to tell tales."

Dora anticipated this issue and made preparations accordingly. She retrieved her handbag from beside her chair, opened the clasp, and pulled out a folded sheet of paper. "Lord Audley sent along a note." Audley had, of course, done no such thing. But Dora always kept a few sheets of his letterhead on file for just such occasions. Before she'd left her house, she'd asked her own maid, Cynthia, who doubled as a forger, to pen a few lines just in case. The note gave Miss Collins his permission to answer all of Dora's questions. "His Grace thought you'd be more comfortable speaking with myself and Miss Kay, rather than Lord Rex. I agreed. Goodness knows, we don't need men prying into the lives of us women." Dora's tart remark earned a smile from Miss Collins. Thus reassured, the maid lowered her cup and asked what they wanted to know.

"What can you tell us about the relationship between Lord and Lady Audley?"

"They got along fine—as well as any other marriage at that level. He had his interests, and she had hers. They usually dined together. I can't remember ever hearing them argue."

"Would you describe Her Grace as happy with her life?"

"Yes..." Miss Collins's voice trailed off.

"I sense a hesitation in there. Please don't hold back. This could be important." Dora softened her gaze and did her best to appear inviting.

"I don't mean to insinuate Her Grace was unhappy with anything or anyone within the household."

"Of course not," Inga agreed. "We aren't interested in casting aspersions or reading into things that aren't there. Tell us what you saw, and we'll figure out whether it is relevant together."

Miss Collins gnawed on her lower lip. Dora hardly dared to breathe. She was on the cusp of something, but one wrong move would send the maid running, letter or not.

Finally, Miss Collins reached a decision. She took a deep breath and sat back, no longer on the edge of making a dash out. "Her Grace was very proper. She was not the type to cross the lines between social classes, but I was the only one in the house whom she brought along. The housekeeper, butler, and other below stairs servants had all worked there for the previous generation. I suspect that is the only reason she trusted me with the task."

"What task?" Dora asked.

"Ferrying messages. Before you ask, I didn't read any of them. I followed her instructions and brought them to the post.

The address was always the same—a postal box in Westminster."

"Do you recall the number?" Inga asked.

Miss Collins shook her head. "If I did, the knowledge got lost over the years. I'd be afraid to hesitate a guess. I'd more likely give you a hat size than the right one."

Dora lifted her teacup to cover her mouth. She didn't want Miss Collins to see her frustration.

"Did the mystery person ever reply?" Inga asked, even though they knew the answer. Audley discovered the letters in his wife's trunk.

"'They did, but not through me. Lady Audley would come home from a night out with an envelope tucked into her pocket. She'd ask me to fetch a copy of the previous day's front page. I never understood why. She'd barely glance at it before sending me away with it again."

Dora knew enough about cryptography to guess the motive behind Lady Audley's request. Somewhere on the front page was the key to decoding the message. She'd tell Caledonia, but she wasn't sure that would be much help. Even if they landed upon the correct dates, how would they determine which word was the code?

Miss Collins picked up her napkin and cleaned her fingers. "I should get back. I stepped out while my mistress is away, and I must be there when she returns."

"One last question," Dora said, reaching over to stop Miss Collins. "When Her Grace received a message, how did she seem? Was she excited?"

"No. If anything, I'd say fearful."

"But you didn't think them in any way connected to her untimely death?"

"How could I?" Miss Collins asked. "She went riding almost

every day. They said it was an accident. I'm sorry, but I really must go. I hope I've been a help."

Dora and Inga assured her she had been. Neither, however, was certain they spoke the truth. On the walk home, they discussed their thoughts.

"That felt like one step forward and two steps back," Dora muttered.

"I agree. We already knew Lady Audley was exchanging messages. Any one of the men from Lord Audley's list could have rented the postal box in Westminster."

"They all also would have no trouble passing notes to her when she was out at social events." Dora stepped aside to let a mother pushing a pram pass. "And fearful? Was Lady Audley afraid of the contents? The sender? Word of something getting out?"

"More questions for our list. Let's walk faster. I'm keen to see how the men are getting on."

The men, however, had little enough good news to share. Dora and Inga found them in the dining room, sitting around stacks of paper. Mews was curled inside a half-empty box, with his fluffy orange tail hanging over the side. Of the group, the cat was the only one who seemed content.

"Please tell me you made progress while we were out," Dora said.

"I've got good news and bad news," Rex said by way of reply.

Dora groaned again before falling into an empty chair. "You pick which one to say first."

"Clark here has been most helpful. We've compiled a dossier for each of the men. We've got their committee assignments from the time and identified their allies."

"That all sounds good. What's the bad?" Inga asked, while taking a seat beside her husband.

Clark answered, "I've sat through enough of those staid

committee meetings to read between the lines of the recorded notes. There is the usual jostling for position and currying of favour. But there are no signs of a serious skirmish. The Hong Kong agreement and the Spanish American war did not seem to be competing for attention or money."

Dora bit back a curse. "We need another clue. Anything."

In a strange twist of fate, the universe chose that moment to provide. The doorbell pealed. Harris leapt to his feet and hurried to answer. He returned moments later, with Caledonia following behind.

Rex's sister beamed at the group, seemingly oblivious to their collective despair. "I have news, and I couldn't wait!"

"Well, go on then," Inga encouraged her. "Out with it."

Caledonia pulled a piece of paper from her pocket and flourished it in the air. "I decrypted the first letter!"

The weariness fell away from Dora's shoulders. She shot upright, fighting the urge to pull Caledonia into a celebratory embrace. "What does it say? Are you sure it is the first?"

"Not certain, but the content puts it a full month before her death."

"Put us out of our misery, Callie," Rex begged. "Read it to us."

Caledonia cleared her throat. "I took some liberties, but I'm confident this is what it says. *If you value your place in society, meet me at the Wiltshire Ball. In the gardens, near the fountain, just after midnight. Come alone.*"

Chapter 8
The Dowager's Diaries

R ex burst with pride at his sister's accomplishment.
"That's incredible! How did you figure out the key to
decode the message?"

"I didn't. It is more accurate to describe it as a sophisticated
game of trial and error. First, I examine which letters are used
most frequently. For example, in English, the letter e is often
used. From there, I do my best to deduce what the words might
be based on what we know. I don't suppose you had any luck
learning the key?"

"We got a hint, but I doubt it will be of much use," Dora
answered. "Lady Audley sent her lady's maid out for the
previous day's paper anytime she received a message. We
assume that something from the paper provided the code, but
your guess is as good as mine on what that is."

"What do we need the key for?" Rex asked. "You decoded
that message in only a couple of days."

Caledonia held up a hand to stop him. "Don't let my speed
with this one lead you to believe the rest will go as quickly. I hit
upon a streak of luck when I realised it referenced a ball. From
there, I went to Grandmama's old social diaries to check the

events calendar for the two months prior to Lady Audley's death. That's where the trial and error came into play. I made a list of balls from that season, and then plugged away until I found one that fit. That gave me more letters to use, and from there, I filled in the blanks."

"Don't ascribe your success to luck," Clark said, cutting into the conversation. "I speak for all of us when I say that even with the best luck in the world, we couldn't have done what you did. Take your well-deserved praise, I insist."

Caledonia curtseyed while Rex and the others applauded her for her accomplishment. When the room died down, she asked what they intended to do next.

"We need to know who went to the ball. I don't suppose Grandmama's diary included any notes on who attended?" Rex asked.

Caledonia shrugged. "She's almost as bad as whoever sent these messages to Lady Audley. She uses initials and pseudonyms instead of real names."

Rex buried his face in his hands and groaned about the women in his life. "In that case, we need both the diaries and the woman herself. Who's up for a trip to Grandmama's house?"

"Please, take me with you," Clark begged, eyeing the piles of paper still on the table. "Surely I've earned a brief respite from this morning of heavy reading."

"You have indeed," Harris replied. "Inga and I can stay here to put things to rights. I'll get Archie to help me run these papers back to Westminster."

"In that case, I'll go along with the men," Dora said. "Clark, do you mind if we go in your car?"

"Not at all. Caledonia, we can give you a lift back home."

"I'll ring Edith, so she knows to expect you," Inga offered.

With that, the group split into two, with Rex, Dora, Clark, and Caledonia travelling across London to the Mayfair mansion the Dowager Duchess called home. Rex sat up front with Clark and soon regretted his hasty decision to let the women take the rear. Clark drove the way he lived, with a casual insouciance that sharpened only a split-second before he risked utter disaster.

In their younger days, before they left for war, Clark's driving abilities raised raucous cheers and calls to go faster. Now Rex knew all too well that no man was immortal. He begged Clark to pay attention to the cars, buses, and wagons weaving through the streets. It was to no avail. Clark did as Clark was want to do. Yet, despite the sharp veers and protests of other drivers, they arrived in one piece.

When they got out of the car, Rex observed a green tint to his sister's features. He hurried over to make sure all was well.

Caledonia sucked in air, desperately searching to steady her nerves. "Remind me never to ride with Clark again. Where on earth did he learn to drive?"

"I don't think he did. It is more that he sprang into the driver's seat with an overwhelming amount of confidence and never looked back."

"Never looked back, indeed. Nor looked left, right, at the traffic signs..." Caledonia shuddered again.

Rex took heart at knowing at least one member of his family wasn't addicted to adrenaline. Lord Audley could tempt his sister all he liked, but if he intended to put her in harm's way, Caledonia was very likely to turn him down on the spot.

"Come along, you two," Dora called. She and Clark hurried to the door, which the Dowager's butler, Sheffield, had already opened.

"Good morning, Lord Clark, Lord Reginald, and Miss Laurent. And welcome back, my lady. Your grandmother awaits you in the library. She wanted me to ask if you intend to remain for luncheon."

Rex glanced at the others. When no one shook their head, he answered, "We might as well. I can't imagine this will be a quick task."

"Excellent, my lord. I will inform the cook."

Rex led the way to the library, where they found his grandmother seated at the central reading table. Rex couldn't help but remember his first murder investigation. He, Dora, Clark, and his grandmother had sat at this very same table, working together to find a killer hiding amongst London's elite. He'd had no idea then that his life was undergoing a vast transformation, taking him from privileged playboy to undercover spy. Yet, despite all the changes, he could still count upon the same people.

"Come in and sit down," Lady Edith said without getting up from her chair. She was well prepared for their arrival. She'd retrieved her social diaries from the year in question and begun the work of refreshing her memory. "I'm afraid I'll be of little use to you. 1898 was not a particularly memorable year of my life."

Caledonia wagged a finger at her grandmother. "Grandmama! How can you say such a thing? You had dozens of events in your social calendar. Not a one of them stands out against the backdrop of time?"

"That's terrible of me to admit, but you must understand. Life was drastically different back then. Unlike your generation, we weren't free to cavort with all levels of society, or swan about town from one club to another."

Rex pulled out a chair for Dora and then took the one beside her. Caledonia sat beside their grandmother, leaving Clark to sit at the end of the table. "You make a fair point. If we're to make headway in this case, we need to remedy our lack of awareness about how society worked. Will you take pity on us poor, young things and provide us with a history lesson?"

"Only because you asked nicely," Edith replied. "Let me see. First, Victoria was queen, which you must recall. She was ancient by then and rarely took part in public life. She despised change, but there we were, on the cusp of a new century. Every week, there was some invention being lauded in the papers."

She turned to Caledonia and Rex. "Your grandfather was still alive then. Clarence detested getting trussed up, as he called it, for the costume balls, musicales, and suppers. He passed that sentiment on to your father and brother. Thankfully, you two took after me."

Clark was aghast. "How could anyone prefer country life over all London has to offer?"

"Indeed. I spent much of my time in London on my own, while Clarence invented excuses for why he needed to remain at the estate. He was so enamoured of you grandchildren that he didn't want to stray. Eventually, however, he'd wonder what I was doing, and he'd take the train to London to find out."

"If your calendar is any example, you were up to plenty," Caledonia said, smiling at her grandmother.

"I had the honour of being a popular guest, because I kept an open mind when making judgments about people. You must remember that at the time, London was awash with American funds. Many of our noble families found themselves to be rich in land and honour, but low in funds. Mothers and fathers of American debutantes saw a unique opportunity to buy their way into the British upper class."

Rex took great care not to glance at Dora. Her mother had arrived in London in the 1890s with just such a purpose. She'd been exceptionally lucky to find someone who wanted her for who she was rather than for the dowry she possessed.

It was an excellent reminder that Dora's father wasn't the only one with connections to the United States. Rex would have to remember to check the extended families of the other men on Lord Audley's list of suspects.

"What about Lady Audley? Was she popular, as well?" Dora asked.

"I remember when she was still Lady Daphne. Lady Arrington had such high hopes for her daughter, but even she never dared to dream she'd wed the heir to a dukedom. I must say that I wasn't surprised. Lady Daphne carried herself well, conversed on any number of topics, and most importantly, made everyone around her feel comfortable. For the wife of a future political leader, that last was an important trait."

"What were your first thoughts when you learned of Lord Audley's suspicions that her death wasn't an accident?"

"Shocked, much as I expect he was. Lady Daphne's death was a terrible tragedy. It felt as though all of London had turned out for her funeral. If there'd been even a hint of doubt about the cause of her death, it would have sat in the headlines for weeks." Edith bowed her white head and took a moment to honour the woman's memory. "Now that I've seen the old letters and read the decoded message, I understand why Lord Audley asked for your help. If someone killed Lady Audley, they got away scot free. I shiver at the thought of a murderer walking among us for so long."

Rex reached over and grasped his grandmother's hand. Her pale skin was paper-thin and dotted with age spots. Yet, her grip remained as firm as ever. Only a fool would count her out because of her age.

"Let us turn our attentions to the night of the ball in question. Did you find anything in your social diaries about the Wiltshire Ball of 1898?" Dora asked.

"Yes, I did. If you'll bear with me a moment, I'll turn to the right page." Edith opened the old leather-bound journal sitting atop the stack of books. She'd marked the page with a strip of lace. "Here we are. Wiltshire Ball, attended by one hundred of London's top families. It was unseasonably warm, leading me to abandon my plan to go as Queen Elizabeth in favour of the goddess Venus. Perhaps that was why I had love on my mind."

"Ohh, matchmaking! Do tell," Caledonia begged.

"You mistake my purpose, dear girl. Lady Tilbury asked me to play chaperone for her daughter. The girl made moon eyes at every passing suitor. It took all my wits and plenty of threats to keep her from ruining herself in the gardens. Believe me, I gave her a stern comeuppance during the carriage ride home." Edith's scowl made everyone laugh.

"Which daughter is that?" Dora asked, fluttering her lashes at the older woman.

"The girl married well in the end, so I shall carry the secrets of her past misdeeds to my grave. They are not relevant. What might be relevant, and I use the word might very loosely in this case, is a note I made regarding Lady Audley. I observed her as she guided Lady Ketchum around and made introductions to some of the other women in her circle.

"Lady Ketchum?" Rex scrunched his brow, but no matter how hard he concentrated, no face swam into view.

"Another of the Americans," Edith supplied. "Perhaps she and Daphne attended finishing school together, or had some other similar connection. Do with that information what you will."

Rex was happy to take any lead, even a tenuous one. "Thanks, Grandmama. We'll figure out some way to approach her. The hard part will be doing so without revealing why we're there."

Dora's face brightened. "I have an idea."

Chapter 9
Tea for Two

After lunch, Dora and Rex hurried to the library to make use of Edith's telephone. Rex gave the operator the number for the Cavendish residence. When someone answered the line, he asked to speak with Lord Benedict.

"Benedict, old chap, is that American cousin of yours still in town?" Rex asked.

"Yes..." Benedict's voice betrayed his suspicion. "Why do you ask?"

"I don't suppose you could ask her whether she's acquainted with Lady Ketchum."

"I am willing to pose the question, but I've got one condition."

Dora rolled her eyes at Rex. Her brother played the role of dutiful heir well, but given half a chance, he loved to try his hand at a little espionage.

"Yes, you can come along. Or even better, you could act as host. Perhaps for tea, today?"

"Consider it done. I'll ring back if I encounter any difficulties with the arrangements. Otherwise, we'll expect you at four."

Dora gave Rex a wide grin. "I told you he'd be game."

"I never doubted you for a moment, darling woman." Rex rewarded Dora with a deep kiss until a harrumph from the doorway interrupted them.

"If you two are quite done, would you mind telling me what Lord Benedict said?" Clark asked.

"He offered to play host," Dora said, skirting the truth.

This was, by far and away, the most troublesome part of having Clark working at their side. He stood at the edge of the shadows, half aware of their existence but not yet clear of how much they hid. Thus far, he'd acquitted himself brilliantly, rising to the occasion as she and Rex expected. But moments such as this one, where Dora had to hide her connection to her family, reminded her of how much was still left unsaid.

Oblivious to Dora's concerns, Clark's moustache quirked up as he gave them a satisfied smile. "Miss Carnegie was rather amusing. If naught else, it won't be hard to spend another hour in her presence."

Dora raised an eyebrow. "Clark Kenworthy, has the American girl caught your eye?"

"No," he replied, shaking his head. "She's far too young for my tastes. But she is good for a laugh, and given what we're up against, I'll take whatever amusement I can get."

"Fair point," Rex conceded. "Seeing as we have a gap in our diaries, can I interest you in a game of billiards?"

"Go on," Dora encouraged him. "I'm sure I can convince Edith to play a few hands of cards. Time spent outwitting an opponent is never wasted."

The trio kept that same mindset while walking to the Cavendish manse. They timed their arrival to be a few minutes early, which turned out to be a fortunate decision. When they walked into the blue drawing room, they found Lady Cavendish waiting like a bird on a fence. She leapt to her feet at their arrival.

Normally, Dora avoided being in close quarters with too many members of her family, where their similarities were bound to be noticed. But today, Dora found her mother's presence to be a boon.

"Good afternoon, your grace," Dora said, bowing her head to her mother. "What a pleasant surprise."

"Please, Theodora, I've asked you to call me Adaline. Benedict mentioned you were on your way, and I thought to show you the new gown I told you about when we had dinner at Lady Rockingham's home."

Dora's mother had made no such mention of a gown, or fashion at all while at the dinner. If her mother wanted to get her alone, she was happy to play along.

"What a fabulous idea! I've been desperate to see it since hearing your description."

Dora winked at Rex as she breezed past and hurried up the main staircase behind her mother. True to her word, Lady Adaline directed Dora to her bedroom suite. She ushered Dora inside and closed the door firmly behind her.

"Why are we having Lady Ketchum over for tea? Has she done something wrong?"

"Not that I am aware. We need to speak with her about the Wiltshire Ball... in 1898."

"The Wiltshire Ball? The costumed affair?"

"That's the one." Dora stopped to inspect her mother's expression. "Were you there?"

Lady Adaline scowled at her daughter. "I most certainly was not. During the summer of 1898, I was at home with a certain newborn daughter. The last thing on my mind was dressing up as a shepherdess and taking part in the country dances until dawn."

"Fair point," Dora conceded, not that she'd expected a different reply. In fact, she'd been hinging her hopes that such an answer would allow them to clear her father's name without having to force him to submit to interrogation. "Lord Audley has us looking into an old matter from around that time."

"Oh?" Lady Adaline's gaze slipped sideways as she did the calculations. Her brow furrowed, and then she pursed her lips into a sad frown. "His wife? Oh! Surely not?"

Dora nodded. "New information has come to light. We're retracing her steps and believe the Wiltshire Ball was important, and Lady Ketchum may know why."

"In that case, I'll stick around for tea. Lady Ketchum never fully settled in here in London. Having a fellow American of her own age in the room may loosen her tongue. If you can find a way to turn the conversation to talk of balls, I'll bring up the Wiltshire event and see what we can pry from her memories."

Dora rushed over and threw her arms around her mother. "Thank you!"

"You're quite welcome, although I hardly think this warrants such appreciation."

Dora pulled back and met her mother's gaze. "Thank you for staying home during the 1898 season. That daughter of yours is one very lucky girl."

"She is indeed," Lady Adaline replied. She pulled free of Dora's embrace and then tweaked her daughter's nose. "Speaking of children, we should rejoin the others. Benedict will have my head if I leave him in charge of hosting afternoon tea. He says it is a woman's affair."

"The more he ages, the more he stays the same," Dora groaned.

Lady Adaline chuckled, but more importantly, didn't disagree. "Don't worry. Since we're all together, I'll be sure to sit on the far side of the room."

The Cavendish drawing room evoked thoughts of the first blooms of spring, regardless of the season. Robin's egg blue silk covered the walls. Fresh flowers bloomed in porcelain vases dotted around the room. The afternoon guests sat upon settees and chairs upholstered in shades of pale green, lavender, and yellow that called to mind fresh shoots of grass interspersed with bellflowers and begonias.

Miss Carnegie was the first to spot them. The Cavendish cousin from the other side of the pond sprang from her chair and hurried over to say hello to Dora.

Dora found the woman's exuberance to be a breath of fresh air compared to the stuffy nature of London's upper class set. She trilled off several compliments in French and kissed the woman on both cheeks before taking her place next to Rex on a settee.

True to her word, Lady Adaline chose a chair on the far side, near Lady Ketchum. After greeting her guest, she made the introductions. "Lady Ketchum, are you acquainted with Miss Laurent? We've had the good fortune of getting to know her at events at the Rockingham's home."

Lady Ketchum's eyes widened as she understood the subtext. Despite her reputation, Dora was in Lady Edith's good graces. No one wanted to be on the dowager's bad side.

"It is lovely to meet you. And thank you, Lady Cavendish, for inviting me over. I haven't seen Miss Carnegie in years."

The footmen arrived bearing trays of tea and cakes. Dora was delighted to find a plate of her favourite cucumber, mint, and cream cheese sandwiches. Knowing her as he did, Rex plated three without asking and passed them her way.

While they enjoyed the food, Dora directed the conversation in the right direction. "Miss Carnegie, has London lived up to your expectations thus far?"

The young woman bobbed her head. "Look at me, having

tea with real lords and ladies! Short of meeting the king, I'm not sure what else I could hope to experience."

"Yes, I often feel the same way," Dora confessed. "However, I must admit I wish I could go back in time and attend one of the famous balls of the social season. Imagine us in fancy ballgowns and elaborate headdresses, with dance cards dangling from our wrists."

"And you and Lord Rex here sneaking off into the garden every time your chaperone turns their head," Clark added, earning a laugh from everyone else.

Rex took the ribbing with good nature. "Can you blame a chap for wanting to corner the attentions of such a fair companion?"

Dora bit the inside of her cheek to keep from laughing at the sour expression on her brother's face.

Miss Carnegie was completely charmed and warmed straight away to the topic. She peppered Lady Ketchum and Dora's mother with questions about their first seasons in London, and how things had changed over the years.

Dora sat back and studied Lady Ketchum. The woman was bone thin and soft-spoken. Her light brown hair was slowly greying, attesting to her middle age. Unlike Miss Carnegie, Lady Ketchum remained hesitant to speak up. She didn't enter the conversation fully until Lady Adaline encouraged her to do so.

Despite her initial hesitancy, she gradually opened up, made more at home by the number of foreigners in the room. Rex, Clark, and Benedict showed no signs of finding her wanting simply because she wasn't British.

"Do you remember the costume balls?" Lady Adaline asked. "The Wiltshires held one in the early summer."

Miss Carnegie gasped in delight. "Tell me all about them. What kinds of costumes did people wear? Did you really put on masks? How could you tell anyone apart?"

"Some couples always went in the same costume, so they were easiest to identify," Lady Adaline replied. "In the cold and rainy years, I was always grateful for the excuse to don extra layers. What about you, Lady Ketchum?"

"They were amongst my favourite events, in part because they felt so freeing. Gone were the titles and formal addresses. Instead, we all played parts in strange, fanciful scenes. Where else would you spot Marie Antoinette, Cleopatra, and Helen of Troy in deep conversation?"

"Indeed. Although, they weren't always such fun, especially when we had a heat wave. Remember the summer of 1898? It was unseasonably warm that year. I was at the country house with a newborn and counted my blessings that I wasn't trapped in a stuffy ballroom. Did you go to the Wiltshire ball that year?"

Lady Ketchum's brow creased. "I must have. The years run together."

"That's true, but 1898 sticks out in my mind, and not just because it is the year my daughter was born. Lady Audley's accident was that summer. She was always so lovely. I hated that I'd missed that time with her."

Dora didn't shift her gaze from Lady Ketchum. Expressions flicked across her face so fast Dora had trouble identifying them. Was that sadness or pain?

Lady Ketchum recovered before Dora could decide. "Yes, I recall now. She was kind to me that evening. I often wondered why she chose to take me under her wing. She died before I had the chance to ask."

The sombre topic cast a pall over the room. Even Dora struggled to find a way to pose more questions to their guest. At her side, Rex shifted uncomfortably, echoing her sentiments.

Miss Carnegie leapt into the silence, redirecting the topic onto safer ground. The conversation moved on to talk of the royal wedding and palace visits. When the clock struck the hour, Lady Ketchum proclaimed it time for her to depart.

She thanked Lady Adaline for hosting and hugged Miss Carnegie goodbye. To Dora she offered a polite handshake.

Dora, Rex, and Clark didn't linger. They still had a case to solve and needed a new lead to follow after this one failed to pan out.

Fortunately for all involved, Dora had come up with an idea. It was a wild hare, at best, and the men were sure to disapprove. But, it was the only option on the table.

Chapter 10
A Trip to Bloomsbury

"Chin up, men. I know somewhere else we can turn for insight," Dora announced once they exited the Cavendish house. "But to access it, I'm going to need to run an errand. Why don't you go on ahead without me?"

Rex recognised that tone of voice as the one she employed when she was covering her tracks. What was she up to now?

He pinned her with a challenging gaze. "Might I have a word before you go?"

Ever good natured, Clark walked ahead a few paces to give them some privacy, and then glanced around as though he were admiring the architecture.

Rex turned his back on his friend. "Where are you going? What is this idea of yours?"

"I'll answer your question with one of my own. Who always seems to know who is canoodling in the shadows?" She wiggled her eyebrows. "And who has access to vast resources about society movements?"

Rex scrunched his brow. She couldn't mean...

"Yes, I can see you've got it — our new friend who just happens to be a gossip columnist. I don't dare make the arrangements on the telephone line. Too much risk of being overheard. So I thought, why not stop in for a visit to see how Prudence is getting on since her return?"

Rex scowled. "Prudence is far too young to have knowledge of an event a quarter of a century ago."

"True, but she must have learned the art of social commentary from someone. I'm willing to bet she can find a way to get us what we need."

"Assuming she is willing to help you again, how will you explain your request?"

"I won't," Dora replied. "I will negotiate a trade, just as I did before. Now, hurry along before poor Clark gets a crick in his neck from staring up at the pigeons perched on the rooftops."

It was pointless to stand in Dora's way once she had an idea in her head. Rex brushed a kiss across her forehead. "We'll wait at Grandmama's instead. Her house is closer."

He watched her saunter away, his gut roiling in dissatisfaction. He didn't like her idea, however brilliant she thought it was. They had far too many secrets of their own to risk spending time in close quarters with a professional gossip.

The problem was that he lacked a better suggestion of where to turn next.

The pair had encountered Prudence Adams during their trip to Italy. There, their search for a killer had led them to uncover a second secret. Prudence wasn't just a member of England's upper class. She was also the woman behind the pen name of London's most famous society columnist.

When Dora had told him of her discovery, Rex had trouble believing it. The evidence, however, was overwhelming.

Dora had used that information to convince Prudence to help them catch a killer. Although Prudence had shown a willingness to trade favours with the pair, this time was different. The secret in question didn't belong to Dora and Rex, but to Lord Audley. The only thing staying Rex's hand at that moment was his implicit trust of his wife.

Rex forced his feet to move along the pavement. Clark fell into step at his side. He was gentleman enough not to pry. That didn't mean Rex did not owe him an explanation.

"Theodora has gone to call in a favour. If it plays out, we'll have a new avenue to explore."

"And if it does not?"

"Good question. That is why we've split up. You and I are going back to my grandmama's to see if she has any other suggestions."

The men found the Dowager Duchess's house empty of all but the servants. Caledonia was off at a lesson and Edith at her modiste. At loose ends, Rex and Clark returned to the games room for another round of billiards.

Rex was down by two games with he heard the trill of the telephone coming from the room next door. Sheffield, the butler, answered and then called Rex to the telephone. "It is Miss Laurent, my lord."

"Darling, we're in luck. Can you be a dear and come collect us?" Dora rattled off an address before ringing off.

Clark's eyebrows crawled up to his hairline. "The Adams house? What is Theodora doing there?"

Rex gave Clark a rough sketch during the drive over. "Prudence has some unusual contacts. It is best if you don't ask too many questions, since she is helping us."

Clark blinked a few times and then shook his head. "Until a few months ago, I never gave Prudence a second thought. Now, I'm realising that was a mistake. The woman is an enigma."

He had no idea...

Dora and Prudence hurried out to the car when Clark pulled up. Dora's red-gold curls drew all eyes away from Prudence's light brown, straight cut. The women had similar figures. But where Dora's clothing was designed to catch attention, Prudence's dull shades did just the opposite. For the first time, Rex grasped why Prudence dressed the way she did. Where Dora paraded through the spotlight, Prudence observed all from behind the curtains.

Rex exited the car and held the door open for Dora and Prudence to slide into the rear seat. After exchanging hellos, Prudence directed them to an address in Bloomsbury.

"Mr Stanley has agreed to see us on one condition," she added.

"What is that?" Rex asked, bracing himself for the reply.

"You are not to ask how he came by anything he shares. His sources will remain secret, no matter how out of date they are."

The request was painless, and Dora, Clark, and Rex agreed without hesitation.

Prudence explained that Mr Stanley lived on the second floor of a three-story walk-up, in the middle of Woburn Walk. Clark found a place to park the car, and the foursome proceeded on foot.

Woburn Walk was a charming pedestrianised street, known for its picturesque and historic atmosphere. Georgian-style buildings lined the pavement, characterised by elegant facades and large windows.

Cafes and small shops filled the ground floors of the buildings, with their glossy black painted exteriors drawing in visitors to sample their wares. The upper floors shone in bright white. The architecture reminded Rex of Belgravia, where Dora had her townhouse. When he mentioned this, Dora explained that both areas shared the same architect. Thomas Cubitt left his mark on London, designing various neighbourhoods along with the east front of Buckingham Palace.

The street had a relaxed ambiance, making it a pleasant place for a leisurely stroll or a quiet afternoon of shopping. Rex had spent precious little time in the area, but knew it was popular with the artist set. From time to time, he and Dora would attend a party at the Strachey home, to rub shoulders with the literati. But an afternoon walk like this was certainly a rarity.

Clark's head swivelled left and right as he looked around with a wondrous gaze. Apparently, Rex was not the only one unfamiliar with this part of town.

Soon enough, Rex turned his attention back to the women in their company. Dora and Prudence walked arm-in-arm ahead of the men. Their heads bent close as they chatted in a low tone. Was it any wonder they had found a certain camaraderie?

They got along like two peas in a pod now, but what would happen if they found themselves on opposite sides of the same issue? Rex shivered at the thought. Although he had full faith in Dora's ability to come out on top of any situation, only a fool would underestimate Prudence.

Prudence came to a stop outside a busy barbershop and turned to face the group. "Mr Stanley worked for the Sunday Pictorial for many years. In his capacity there, he built an impressive personal archive based on the whispers around town. To this day, journalists still consult him."

"And you know this man?" Clark asked. "Wait, never mind. Don't answer that."

Prudence gave him a side-eyed gaze before shifting to take his full measure. In his custom-tailored suit and shiny Italian loafers, he was every inch a gentleman. Beneath his thick moustache peeked a sheepish smile. Clark had a reputation for getting up to no good, but there wasn't an evil bone in his body. Rex suspected much of his shenanigans came out of boredom. Clark rarely had a chance to make full use of his clever mind, outside of inventing his renowned elaborate scavenger hunts.

If Rex and Dora had their way, all that would change. Clark

would be catapulted headfirst into the twisty world of half-truths and lies where men like Lord Audley reined supreme.

What did Prudence see? She had to be gifted at seeing below the surface, reading body language, and sizing up a man. Rex grew tense the longer she remained quiet.

Finally, she spoke. "Yes, Lord Clark, I am acquainted with Mr Stanley. After today, you will be as well. Please don't make me regret arranging this introduction."

Clark dropped his grin and squared his shoulder. In a serious voice, he replied, "You have my promise that I will be on my best behaviour."

Prudence nodded her approval and led them to a small doorway next to the barbershop. She pressed on the appropriately labelled bell and waited to be let inside.

A portly man, barely more than five feet tall, opened the door and smiled in delight upon seeing Prudence. "Miss Adams, it has been too long," he said in a croaky voice. "And you've brought guests along. Please, follow me upstairs and we'll do the introductions without half the neighbourhood watching."

Despite the man's diminutive height, he hurried up the stairs and through a door on the second floor. He bade them all to come inside and make themselves at home.

"Mr Stanley, I present Lord Clark, Lord Rex, and Miss Laurent." Prudence glanced at the others. "As you can guess, this is Mr Stanley."

Mr Stanley shook the men's hands in turn, offering a firm grip and a scrutinising eye. Although the man's gaze didn't linger, Rex had the sensation he'd been measured from top to bottom. Mr Stanley kept his opinion to himself as he hurried to reach Dora. Only then did he show his admiration.

"Miss Laurent, it is truly an honour to have you as a guest in my home. Had I known Miss Adams was a shared acquaintance, I'd have demanded she bring you by sooner."

Dora adopted her favourite femme fatale pose, with a hand on one hip and a sly smile on her face. "I bet you say that to all the women who feature regularly in the society columns. Tell me the truth, Mr Stanley. Do I live up to my reputation?"

Mr Stanley barked a laugh. "You exceed it, by miles, as you well know. Now, have a seat and tell me what it is you need from a poor man like me."

Despite his words, Mr Stanley lived in a spacious, sunlit flat. The reception room featured sturdy furniture with clean lines and fine upholstery. Books filled the shelves lining one wall, stacked willy nilly, with no obvious order. The collection ran the gamut from Shakespeare to Dickens and on through to DH Lawrence and James Joyce. The artwork on the walls all held to a single theme. Whether it be an old photograph or an oil portrait, every picture included at least one person. Mr Stanley was a man fascinated not so much by the world around him as the other people living in it.

Prudence motioned for Dora to take the lead.

"Mr Stanley, we come to you with a most strange request. In May 1898, the Wiltshires held their annual costume ball. We believe someone held an illicit meeting in the gardens that night. Miss Adams said you, and only you, might still hold a record of anything out of the ordinary that happened at the event. Can you shed any light on our question?"

Mr Stanley tapped his chin. "Perhaps... But such information comes with a price."

Rex bit back a groan.

Dora, however, was unfazed. "I expected no less. What can I offer in trade?"

"A dinner invitation."

"Done."

"Not so fast," Mr Stanley challenged. "It isn't your home I

wish to visit. I ask that you arrange for me to dine with Lady Rockingham."

"Grandmama?" Rex blurted. "Why her?"

"Because she is the only person from my heyday who came close to equalling my underground whisper network. Should she be willing, I am certain we would find plenty about which to converse."

Rex covered his face with his hand.

"Is that a no?" Mr Stanley asked, his croaky voice souring in disappointment.

"Far from it," Dora answered before Rex could jump in. "We don't even need to ring and ask. I am confident she will be happy to play hostess for just such a night. If you can provide us with some convenient dates, we will check her diary and telephone you later tonight with a firm plan."

Mr Stanley's face lit up in satisfaction. "Wait here, while I consult my notes."

He disappeared through another doorway leading to a corridor. Faint sounds of sliding boxes floated from the other room. In a thrice, Mr Stanley returned with a folded page in hand. He went to his desk and took pen and paper. Under the watchful gaze of his guests, he scribbled a few lines of text on a page.

He offered both items to Dora. "Here is the guest list and the names of the individuals spotted in the gardens that night — something my informant believed was beyond simply going out for air. If you can leave the guest list with Lady Rockingham after you review it, I can collect it when I come for dinner."

Dora took the items, holding them as though they were precious treasures. To her, they were.

Mr Stanley returned to his seat and asked if they had time to stay for a drink. They were hardly in a position to say no. He poured gin and lime juice into five glasses and topped them with soda water. While they sipped their Gin Rickeys, he peppered them with questions about the fresh faces on the social circuit.

By the time they said their goodbyes, Rex was no longer certain who'd got the better end of that deal. The guest list and gossip well exceeded his expectations for the visit, but they'd paid twice over in return. Not only had they promised dinner with his grandmama, they'd also given Mr Stanley plenty of new information for his archives.

Chapter 11
Fears are Faced

For Dora, patience wasn't so much a virtue as a skill gained through years of practice. She exercised that skill while riding in the back seat with Prudence. The other woman eyed her, her gaze slipping from Dora's face to the handbag where Dora had tucked Mr Stanley's note. It was a competition of wills for both of them. Prudence could not ask. Dora would give no hint.

After they dropped Prudence back at her home, all that changed. Dora instructed Clark to go to her house, where they would regroup with Harris and Inga. She waited until the men got caught up in a conversation before quietly pulling the note out to read.

Mr Stanley had written six names on the page - Lord and Lady Ketchum, Sir William Church, Miss Maeve Finch, Lady Audley, and one more that caused Dora's Audley stomach to drop.

Lord Cavendish.

Was this why Lady Ketchum had seemed pained during the discussion of the masquerade ball? Had she stumbled across a compromising situation? If so, she'd held her tongue for all these years.

Dora's mind raced through the possibilities. She paid no notice to the men, only returning to the present when Clark stopped the motorcar. Without a word of explanation, she handed the guest list to Rex and then hurried from the car.

Inga was sitting in the drawing room when Dora came in. She glanced up, caught sight of Dora's pale face and pinched lips, and rose without a word. She followed fast on Dora's heels as she went upstairs.

Dora had one destination in mind. She made a beeline for the privacy of her bedroom, a space where few would follow. Once inside, she walked across the room until she reached the window overlooking the narrow garden behind her conservatory.

"Bad news?" Inga asked from the other side of the room.

Staring out the window, Dora sucked in air to gain control over her spiralling emotions. She discovered she was unable to speak, thus she simply inclined her head in confirmation to Inga's question.

"Sit. We will talk this through," Inga said in a harsh voice that brooked no argument.

Wordlessly, Dora turned around and trod to the small sitting area near the empty fireplace. She pulled the note out and handed it to Inga. "These are the people spotted in the gardens on the night of the Wiltshire Ball."

Inga read the note and then folded it again and again until she hid it in the palm of her hand. "It isn't just this, is it?"

Dora told Inga about the visit to her parents' home and the conversation with Lady Ketchum. After she finished, she buried her face in her hands. "What if I am wrong about him?"

"You aren't."

Dora lifted her head. "How can you sound so sure? Even

Lord Audley was willing to consider the possibility. Otherwise, why put him on the list?"

"Lord Audley only knows your father as an adversary. It is easy for his mind to drift further that way. You know your father is a good man."

"Do I, though? Most of my recollections are through a child's rose-coloured lens. My interactions with him as an adult are so limited."

"Yet telling, nonetheless. How did your father react when Audley recruited you to his spy network? What of all the times you've been in danger here? And your relationship with Rex - has your father ever threatened him for taking up with you before you wed?"

Inga's questions penetrated the haze of fear clouding Dora's mind.

"Send Rex to question him if you must."

Dora shook her head. "No, I will go. I have never fallen prey to my fears before, and I will not do so now. I will go alone after dark."

"Very well. What now? Did you learn anything else of use?"

"We got a copy of the guest list. I left it with Rex and Clark, who must be downstairs wondering what has become of me." Dora shook off her worries and pasted a smile across her face. "Come. We should join them."

The women descended the stairs together. Rex and Clark were in the drawing room with Harris, reviewing the longer list of names. They glanced up, wearing matching expressions of concern.

"Apologies," Dora said. "I recognised the name of a longstanding acquaintance on the list and needed a moment to reflect on it."

"Was it the only name listed?" Rex asked.

"No." Dora grabbed a pencil from the side table and took the list. She placed a mark next to the other names.

"None of these people are on Lord Audley's list of suspects," Clark pointed out.

"Indeed. It will take time for us to learn about them. Given the hour, I suggest we break for dinner and regroup tomorrow morning."

"I must make my excuses," Clark said, rising from his chair. "I accepted a dinner party invitation before all this began. Unless you want me to send my apologies."

"There is no need. It is best we keep up the appearance that all is normal, lest people wonder what we are about." Dora kept the faux smile on her face as she waved goodbye.

Rex asked no questions of Dora. Given her behaviour, he suspected she had left a name off the list, and there was only one past acquaintance who would cause her so much heartache. He did not need an explanation of why she had not told Clark that her father's name had been included. He trusted her to deal with the situation as she saw fit.

In return, she asked him to drive her across town at the appointed hour. Dressed in unassuming black clothing, they climbed into the Model T. Dora told Rex to park beside the stone wall encircling her family's London property.

Not even a year and a half had passed since Harris had parked in the same location, so she could scale the wall and confront her brother. That night had been a game to her. This one, far from it.

Dora squeezed Rex's hand for luck. She waited until a cloud covered the moon, darkening the pavement, and slid from the car. Fast as a cat, she scaled the wall and grabbed hold of a tree limb. She slithered between the leafy branches, grateful that autumn had not yet arrived.

She dropped onto the house grounds and crouched low.

The light in her father's study burned bright. Benedict was ruled out as a possibility, since he had mentioned his opera tickets for that night. Her mother had always preferred her sitting room on the second floor. It had to be Dora's father, working late into the night on some business for the House of Lords.

She stole across the shadowed gardens and peered through the nearest window. She spotted the back of her father's head, bent over papers on his desk, his cigar long since forgotten in the ashtray. Lightly rapping to get his attention, she stifled a grin when he leapt at the sound.

He squinted at the window, searching to see who was out there, his brows creased until he spotted Dora's moonlit face staring back. He undid the latch and pushed it open wide enough for her to climb in.

He turned away and walked across the room, not wanting to watch her contortions. Over his shoulder, he asked, "Have you forgotten that we have doors?"

Dora didn't reply. Sitting as she was, half in and half out, she felt herself on the literal and proverbial precipice. Inside the room, the sweet scent of her father's favourite cigars evoked memories of her childhood days watching him work. Outside, the sharp edge to the night air reminded her that life cut both ways. Darkness hid both the good and the bad. She could turn around and jump back to the ground, running away from the possible hard truth. But one day she would grow tired. What then?

However, she couldn't ignore the fact that moving forward with this plan held risks. Depending on how her father answered her questions, that selfsame cigar scent could turn sour.

Time and again in her life, Dora had faced the tough choices head on. If her father was somehow responsible for Lady

Audley's death, could she live with a decision to turn a blind eye?

That answer, at least, was as clear as a bright summer day.

She swung her legs over and dropped onto the parquet floor. The window slid shut with only a small squeak. She flipped the latch closed, cutting off any thoughts of a quick escape.

Her father had turned to face her again. The only light in the room came from the lamp on his desk. Standing as he was, his face was half-shadowed. His Cavendish green eyes looked like black holes.

"This is not a personal visit, is it?"

Dora shook her head. Her father moved over to the sitting area, choosing his favourite wingback. She claimed the sofa across from him.

"The season of 1898. Did you spend it in London?"

He cocked his head to the side and frowned in confusion. Her mother must not have had a chance to tell him about the motivation for Dora's afternoon visit.

"I'm certain you don't recall, but I was somewhat occupied that year. Rubbing elbows with the upper crust was far down my list."

Dora shifted forward. "You didn't go to any London events at all that year? No balls? No nights at the opera?"

"Why are you asking me this question? What is going on?"

Dora huffed out the breath she'd been holding. "The Wiltshire costume ball. You were there, without Mama. Why?"

Her father rocked back in his chair and scrunched his brow. The date held no immediate significance for him. Was that a sign of his innocence? Dora held tight to the faint spark of hope.

"Yes, I went to that event. I'd honestly forgotten. It was a last-minute decision. I didn't even bother with a costume or a mask."

"Then why did you go?"

"There was a war on between the Americans and the Spaniards. A group of visiting dignitaries wanted my help to plead their case. I originally intended to invite them to a country weekend, but once your mother saw the names of the guests, she insisted I meet them in London instead." Lord Cavendish shook his head and chuckled. "She described one of the men as a hot-headed know-it-all and confessed she'd bloodied his nose once in a childhood scuffle. She couldn't stomach the thought of entertaining him in her home."

Dora wanted to laugh at the story. She'd long suspected she owed her strong will to her mother, rather than her father. But she held tight until she asked her last question.

"Did Lord Audley have anything to do with your meeting? Was he standing in your way?"

"Audley? We're rivals, but that doesn't mean we pick fights over every issue. If I recall correctly, he was busy with something else? The extension of our lease of Hong Kong? Our paths crossed later, once the Americans gained a foothold in Asia, and suddenly he had to find a way to make friends with our cousins across the pond. I don't even know if he was there that night. Or if anyone was! Everyone else had on some ridiculous costume and half-mask. It made finding my contacts a blood-err, ahem, blind challenge."

This was the father she recalled — a man who said what he thought, and lamented about the trappings of the very society from which he benefitted. He wouldn't resort to coded messages and threats if he wanted something from Audley. She'd been a fool to even consider it.

She was back to square one, but she was not going to complain about the lack of progress. Far better to have hit a dead end in this particular case. Without asking permission, she leapt to her feet and helped herself to a glass of Scotch. Her father retrieved his half-empty glass from his desk and held it out for a top up.

After she replaced the stopper in the crystal decanter, she returned to her seat. She raised her glass in a silent toast, smiling when her father copied her gesture.

Lord Cavendish allowed his daughter a single sip before he asked a question of his own. "Did you come here alone, or do you have someone waiting outside?"

"Rex is in the Model T, parked around the corner."

Lord Cavendish rose from his chair and headed towards the bell to summon a servant. A footman arrived with great haste. Cavendish despatched him to retrieve Rex and invite him inside for a nightcap.

"He'd have waited, Papa," Dora assured him after the footman left the room.

"He might, but I won't. I expect a full explanation for why you put me to the inquisition, and I don't want you to have any excuse to make a quick getaway."

Chapter 12
Cocktails at Westminster

T he next morning, Rex, Dora, and Clark gathered again around the dining room table. Once again, Rex's cat had opted to join them, jumping into Rex's lap with a demand to be stroked. The cat purred as Rex led a discussion on how best to search for more information about the names that Mr Stanley had put on his list.

"Lord and Lady Ketchum make for an interesting pair," Clark noted. "You said Mr Stanley was a society columnist. Why would he take note of a married couple out in the garden?"

"Perhaps they had an argument," Rex ventured. "Think about it. Theodora has only to sniff in my direction and the headlines proclaim our love affair at an end."

"Yes, I agree," Dora chimed in. "I kept a close watch on Lady Ketchum's facial expressions yesterday when we spoke about the ball. I'm sure I saw a flash of pain. If she and Lord Ketchum had a big enough row that night, she'd remember."

Clark scratched his chin. "What if they had a row because Lady Ketchum caught her husband alone with Lady Audley?"

Rex and Dora considered the possibility.

Rex spoke first. "We can't rule it out, but Lady Ketchum

showed no signs of bearing Lady Audley any ill-will. She remarked on how kind Lady Audley had been to introduce her to others. Would Lady Audley do that if Lord Ketchum was sending her threatening notes?"

"What if Lady Ketchum was blackmailing Lady Audley? We shouldn't assume the sender of these notes was a man." Dora added, "Women can be just as devious, you know."

Rex and Clark both remained mum, neither wanting to wade into that conversation.

"Very well, we'll keep the pair on the table as possible suspects." Clark moved to the next names on the list. "That leaves us with Sir William Church, Maeve Finch, and Lady Audley. We know why the latter was on her own, but what of the other two?"

"I can answer that one," Inga said, coming through the dining-room door. "Sir William Church was married at the time. When his first wife died during childbirth, he was very quick to marry Maeve Finch. I remember my father being aghast because of Sir William's lack of respect for the proper mourning period. The wedding took place less than three months after his wife's death."

"Your father?" Clark rocked back at this first mention of Inga's family.

"Yes, I have a father. Although he and I are not close. That is all you need to know, Lord Clark." Inga's closed expression stopped him from asking anything else. "Telling you about Sir William was not the only reason I came in. We had a call from Caledonia."

Rex jerked up straight at his sister's name. "Is she coming over? Does she bring news?"

"Her message was succinct enough that she delivered it over the telephone. The second letter is taking her longer to understand, but she has figured out a few words. One of them is affair."

Rex's shoulders dropped. He'd been dreading the possibility he might have to bring bad news to Lord Audley about his wife's fidelity. How would the man react if it turned out that his wife was killed by her spurned lover?

Rex glanced around the table and saw mirroring expressions on the other faces. "Distasteful as this is, we must investigate. Any suggestions on where to start?"

"If we were looking at a recent crime, I'd ask your grandmother or someone like her." Dora frowned. "But we're not. We're bumping up against the same problem. How do we get people to gossip about someone who died twenty-five years ago?"

A pall fell over the table until Inga clapped her hands together. "There are two parties involved, and one of them is still among the living. We don't need people to gossip about Lady Audley. We can needle them for information on the duke, instead."

"Of course!" Dora shot to her feet. "Brilliant, as always. Tell me, men. Are there any upcoming events where we can expect Lord Audley to attend?"

"Edith would know," Inga suggested.

"No need to ring her, old girl," Clark said, cutting in. "If we're free this evening, I have an event that will fit the bill."

Clark had an active social life, to say the least, but Rex couldn't imagine it overlapped with Lord Audley's rare outings. However, his skepticism faded when Clark explained.

"I have invitations to a cocktail reception at Westminster, in honour of visiting dignitaries from Southern Rhodesia. Lord Audley would not dare miss such an event."

"Won't most of the guests be men?" Rex asked.

"Politicians," Clark clarified. "If there is a skeleton in Lord

Audley's closet, they'll know whose it is. It is a point of pride in those circles. There are always a few wives in attendance, so Theodora will not necessarily stick out."

Dora and Inga nodded their agreement. Rex fought a losing battle against the grimace crossing his face. His one foray into the political world had ruined his appetite. He much preferred to pit his wits against foreign enemies than his fellow countrymen.

Clark, he noted, was rubbing his hands together with relish. Since their trip to Rome, Clark had discovered political games could be as interesting a diversion as his legendary scavenger hunts. Rex didn't hold it against him. It was exactly why Rex had suggested Clark's name as Lord Audley's protégé.

Dora announced she needed to go shopping for new shoes, and all but demanded Inga accompany her. Thus inspired, Clark remembered he needed a new pair of cufflinks. Rex waved them all goodbye, opting to spend time with Harris. The two men had become close friends by now, but Rex's busy social schedule and societal constraints limited their opportunities to do something together.

At seven o'clock sharp, Rex and Dora exited their Rolls-Royce in front of Westminster Palace. The statue of Oliver Cromwell looked down upon the pair from its position of honour next to the storied edifice he'd gone to war to defend. It served as a dual reminder of both the independence of Parliament from the king and the risk of brothers taking up arms against one another in a civil war.

Rex pushed such fears from his mind and offered Dora his arm. Together, they presented themselves at the entrance to Parliament. A clerk checked their name against the list and then waved them through the doorway into Westminster Hall. Given the late hour, the hall was empty of tourists and visitors. Rex spotted a few harried clerks leaving after a long day.

Accustomed to the venue hosting after-hours events, they paid Rex and Dora no mind.

At the far end of the hall, they climbed the stairs and turned left into St Stephen's Chapel. Rex cast a glance at his wife, wondering whether she was thinking about the wider history of the room, or the more recent events of barely more than a decade earlier, when a group of suffragettes chained themselves to the statues. Had Dora been older then, Rex had little doubt she'd have led the charge.

However, if such thoughts crossed her mind on this day, she kept them to herself. She played the dutiful consort, smiling politely at all as they passed. They didn't stop until they entered the Central Lobby, where the evening event was being held.

As predicted, most of the hundred or so people milling around were of the male persuasion. Booming voices and hearty laughs filled the air. Dora, however, was not the only woman in attendance. Rex caught flashes of colourful dresses in between the staid black suits. Still, the men outnumbered the women three to one.

Dora spotted Clark across the way and tapped on Rex's arm to get his attention. "Shall we get a drink and say hello to Lord Clark?"

Rex and Dora paused many times along their way, stopping to speak with people who called out a hello. Dora's popularity with the men was both a blessing and a curse. At the moment, it was preventing the couple from reaching Clark. Later on, Rex trusted it would help loosen lips when Dora broached the subject of Lord Audley.

Rex was not sure how to react when he noticed the man himself standing beside Clark. Although they'd counted on Lord Audley's presence at the event, Rex had given little thought to what they'd say to him.

Clark, it seemed, had already taken care of the matter. Lord

Audley greeted Rex and Dora and then took his leave to speak with the other new arrivals.

"We've been invited round for a late supper," Clark explained in a low voice.

"Anything else of which we should be aware?" Rex asked.

"No. We have carte blanche to do whatever is needed to get the answers he wants. I asked him to mill around so that we will have an excuse to bring up his name."

"Then I suggest we split up. We'll take different parts of the room and reconvene near the entrance to St Stephen's Chapel in an hour."

Rex moved toward the Commons Corridor. He stopped to take a glass of champagne from a passing server. When he glanced backward, he saw Dora speaking with Mrs Mabel Phillipson. The former actress turned newly elected MP was a favourite of Dora's, and it was easy to understand why. Both women had heaps of experience operating in a man's world and achieving great success while doing so. Although Mrs Phillipson was unlikely to be helpful with the current matter, Rex hardly resented Dora's decision to stop for a natter.

Rex turned his attention to the nearest man he recognised. Lord Bethell was of a similar age to Lord Audley. Rex sidled over and casually joined the man's conversation with another peer. It was a spot of luck that the man who had been facing away from Rex was none other than Lord Adams, Prudence's uncle.

"Lord Rex, fancy seeing you here. Have you taken a shine to politics?" Lord Bethell asked. "You spoke from the heart last year when you visited the Conservatives leadership elections. We can always use men who are not afraid to speak up."

"Lord Rex is equally capable of holding his tongue," Lord Adams said. "My niece Prudence told me something about the events in Rome. From what I've heard, you were at the forefront of the murder investigation. Yet, you demanded no reward for your effort."

"I was in the right place at the right time," Rex answered. "Lord Clark was the real lead. I merely assisted him."

"You and your lovely paramour, Miss Laurent," Lord Adams said, nodding toward where Dora stood.

"What can I say? If you had a woman half as lovely as Theodora on your arm, wouldn't you do whatever she asked? She said we could hardly abandon Lord Clark, and she was correct. Speaking of women, how are your lovely wives?"

With a steady hand, Rex guided the conversation away from politics and onto the subjects of wives and confidants. When Lord Audley happened by, Rex nodded his way.

"I am surprised a man of his stature never remarried, especially as he has no heir."

"The title will pass to his brother and eventually his nephew, a fine lad currently at Eton." Lord Bethell lowered his voice. "Rumour is that Lord Audley is unable to sire a child. Perhaps that is why he was in no rush to remarry."

"Really?" Rex raised his eyebrows. "Call me a romantic, but I thought it was because of his wife's sudden death."

Lord Adams shook his head. "Though tragic, theirs was hardly a great love story."

He shifted, moving closer to the men. "Was there some suggestion of impropriety?"

Lord Bethell chuckled at Rex's bold question. "Lord Audley's reputation is far from lily white, but it has steadfastly remained free of any serious black marks. He was too intent on gaining power to allow a woman to distract him. Still is."

"What of Lady Audley?"

"She came quietly onto the scene. Audley caught us all off guard when he asked for her hand. He saw something in Daphne that we did not. She proved to be an able partner —

conversant, friendly, and yet with a strong backbone. They understood one another. Likely, that is what made her so hard for Audley to replace." Lord Bethell shook his head. "But enough about such maudlin matters. Let us return to our earlier discussion. Might we make a politician of you yet?"

Rex danced around the topic, seeing the wisdom of not committing himself one way or the other. Who could say what the future held in store, or what roles he might have to play down the line? After a reasonable amount of time, he extricated himself and moved on to repeat variations of the conversation about Lord Audley's past.

Halfway through the event, a man bumped into Rex from behind, hard enough to knock him off balance. Rex glanced over his shoulder, but all he saw was the back of a tall man with brown hair hurrying away. The crowd swallowed him up, making any thought of pursuit impossible. In truth, the event was busy enough that Rex wasn't sure whether the bump had been on purpose or was an accident.

The trip was turning out to be for naught. He heard not one suspicion about Lady Audley's commitment to her husband.

Chapter 13
The Double Meaning

An hour later, Dora, Rex, and Clark exited Parliament. The sun dipped below the horizon and the gas lamps cast their warm glow upon the streets of Westminster. They passed through the iron gates surrounding the grounds and joined the people passing on the pavement. Cars and horse-drawn carts shared space on the cobblestone street, creating a cacophony of growling motors and clip clop of horseshoes.

Near the corner, a young boy called out to passersby, hawking the evening edition of the day's papers. A man in a dapper suit counted change from his pocket and then took the folded paper and tucked it under his arm.

People strolled past the trio, some giving them a second and third glance. Dressed as they were, Rex and Clark in black tie and Dora in a beaded dress, they stood out against the gothic architecture at their backs.

Dora wished she could use one of her usual tricks, shedding her upper class skin in favour of an ill-fitting dress and worn shoes. Given the chance, she'd return to Westminster to search through cupboards and drawers until she found some clue to help them on their way.

But tonight, there was no mystery document or penned note hiding within the towering walls of the British government. The secrets hid in the depth of people's minds, a much harder place to plumb. She put forth her best efforts into her assignment, but she had no tangible results.

"Any luck?" Dora asked. The men shook their heads. Despite conversing with most of the men and women of a similar age to Lord Audley, no one had a cross word to say about Lady Audley or her marriage.

"Another dead end," Clark grumbled. "And now we've got to come clean with Lord Audley about our lack of progress."

"It isn't for want of trying," Dora reminded him. "Perhaps this quote from Thomas Jefferson will improve your mood—"

"Thomas Jefferson? The American?"

"The very same. He said he was a great believer in luck, but added that he found the harder he worked, the more he had of it. So, too, will it be for us. If we turn over enough stones, eventually we'll find something of use."

"Let us hope so." Clark glanced around at the passing traffic. "Shall I flag a taxi for us?"

"No need," Rex answered. "I brought the Rolls. You can ride over with us."

Rex's shiny white Rolls-Royce, with gold trim and tan leather interiors, stood out like a diamond amidst the line of plain black Model Ts. The papers had gone mad when he first took it for a spin around town, catapulting him and Dora to new levels of fame.

Dora was impressed by his forward thinking. It was exactly the sort of misdirection at which she excelled. Keep everyone talking about the things you do in the light so they overlook what happens in the deepest dark of night.

At the mention of the Rolls, Clark sighed in envy. He had

asked several times for a chance to drive the new car, but Rex stood firm in saying no.

For once, it wasn't an argument over who was to drive that stopped them all in their tracks. When Rex opened the car door for Dora to get in, they realised that someone else had already been there. A bouquet of calla lilies lay upon the passenger seat.

"It seems our Theodora has a new fan," Clark said, elbowing Rex. "You will have to step up your efforts if you want to retain her affection."

"My affection does not come this cheaply," Dora replied, putting Clark in his place. She leaned over to pick up the flowers, but came away holding only the stems. The person who left the gift had severed the heads from the bunch. "And it is a good thing, as I do not believe this is meant to curry favour."

"Egads!" Clark exclaimed. "Why would someone leave beheaded flowers in the car?"

Neither Dora nor Rex had an answer. Dora glanced along the pavement, searching the area for any flower sellers. Though there were plenty of passersby, none carried bouquets or called for people to stop. Given their last minute decision to attend the event, it was unlikely someone would have known to find Rex's motorcar parked outside Westminster.

A third possibility crossed Dora's mind. "Whoever did this must have been at the event."

Rex froze in place. "It was no accident," he muttered. Dora raised her eyebrows at him, and he added, "Someone bumped me hard from behind. I did not get a good look at him. All I can tell you was it was a man with brown hair."

She passed Rex her handbag. "There's only one way to know for sure. Wait here. I need to dash back inside."

She did not wait for Rex and Clark to follow. As quick as she could, she hurried along the pavement until she reached the iron gates surrounding the Palace of Westminster. The uniformed guard recognised her.

"Is something wrong, miss?"

"Silly me, I forgot my handbag inside. I don't suppose someone brought it out for me?"

"No. Would you care to go back in to look for it? Or I can take your name and address, and have it sent round later."

"I'm almost certain I left it on a bench in the Central Hall. I'll go make a quick check."

The guard opened the door and waved Dora through. Inside the main hall, she hurried up the stone stairs and through St Stephen's Chapel until she reached Central Hall once again. She made a quick turn about the room, dodging glances so as not to be drawn back into a conversation. She spotted close to a dozen men who fit Rex's description, some she recognised and others she did not. That was a dead end.

She turned her mind to the other avenue of investigation — the floral sprays decorating the tables and pedestals. At the far end of a table holding glasses of champagne and canapés, she spotted the answer to one of her questions.

She retraced her steps out of the palace, and assured the guard she'd asked a clerk to send her missing handbag, should it turn up again. "It was a favourite of mine, but hardly priceless. That will teach me to be so careless."

The guard tipped his hat and waved her goodbye.

Rex and Clark were leaning against the side of the Rolls when she returned.

"I did not find your mystery man, but I can confirm that the flowers came from the cocktail reception," she said. "All the arrangements included calla lilies except for one. We have a new lead, gentleman. I suggest we hurry over to Lord Audley's to make him aware."

While Rex concentrated on navigating through London's

busy streets between Westminster and Mayfair, Dora considered the meaning behind the floral message.

Inga might chastise her for leaping to conclusions, but Dora felt certain that the flowers had to be related to the questions they'd been asking. The problem was that she did not know whether someone overheard them, or if someone lied to their faces and then went out of their way to scare them off the case.

They arrived in Mayfair before Dora reached a conclusion. She suggested Rex turn into the alley behind Lord Audley's mansion and park near the old mews. "Although our visit is not a secret, given what happened, there is no need to advertise where we are."

Lord Audley's ever-efficient butler met them on the back terrace and welcomed them into the house. He guided them to the drawing room where Lord Audley awaited.

Lord Audley instructed the butler to fix the new arrivals a drink and then to let them know when dinner was to be served. After the butler departed, Audley settled into a wingback chair and said, "I realise we are on friendly terms, but guests generally arrive through the front door of the house. What has happened?"

Dora opened her handbag and pulled out a folded handkerchief. She unrolled it on the top of a side table to reveal the stems and flowers from the calla lilies. "We found these in the motorcar when we left."

Lord Audley's face paled. "Calla lilies? Those were Daphne's favourite."

Dora and Rex exchanged worried glances. This message had an even deeper meaning than they'd suspected.

"We have good news and bad news, your grace," Dora said. She folded the cloth over the flowers, wanting them out of their sight. "The good news is that we must have crossed paths with the sender of the cryptic letters. The bad news is that they are now aware of what we are doing. Unfortunately, they are going to be a step ahead."

Lord Audley took the news better than they expected. "Asking questions about someone so long gone was bound to raise a few eyebrows. Tell me, why were you three at the cocktail reception?"

"Caledonia unravelled another clue," Rex said. "She has not yet figured out the full message, but she was certain part of it referenced an affair."

Clark raised his hand. "It was my idea to go tonight and see if we could uncover any old whispers about your wife's fidelity."

"And did you?" Lord Audley braced himself for the worst.

"No, we did not." Clark opened his mouth and closed it again just as fast. Dora guessed at the direction his mind had gone, and why he was hesitant to voice his thoughts.

"Lord Audley, you said we could ask anything of you. Was the message regarding something you did? Were you having an affair? We won't judge," Dora added.

"I was not. I never stepped outside of my marriage. Though I had no doubts, I am relieved to learn it appears neither did my wife." He sipped his drink. "Where does that leave us?"

Dora held out her hands and shrugged. "Back to guessing, at least until Caledonia unscrambles another message. I must admit, I am struggling to make sense of all this. The pieces of information we have do not even seem to be part of the same puzzle."

Dora's words hung in the air, casting a pall over the group. The timely arrival of Audley's butler saved them from having to fill the gap.

"Dinner is served, your grace," he announced. He stepped aside to let Lord Audley and his guests leave the room.

The dining table was long enough to sit twelve comfortably. For this evening, the butler gave instructions to the footmen to set four places at one end. Lord Audley sat at the head of the table, with Clark on his right and Rex and Dora to his left. Dinner was a staid affair, comprising smoked salmon, followed by grilled halibut with potatoes Hollandaise, and finally an apple almond strudel with vanilla and cinnamon ice cream.

The menu was not the only thing fishy. While the others made polite conversation about the latest goings-ons in England's international affairs, Dora kept turning the pieces over in her mind.

She felt certain that the person sending the notes had to have some hold over Lady Audley. They posed a threat to her position in society. What kinds of secrets could lead to her downfall?

Lord and Lady Audley's marriage had not come as the result of a precipitous rush to the altar. They had followed the correct courting procedure, posted their banns, and wed in good time. Furthermore, they had no children, and there was nothing to suggest Lady Audley had not come to the marriage bed with her reputation intact.

Whatever Lady Audley did to put her place in society at risk, must have come after their wedding. Dora and the others assumed that the reference to an affair must have been of the carnal sort. But what if they were off track?

Intimate affairs raised eyebrows if brought into the light. Egregious enough, and they might even warrant discussion of retiring to the country, or worst cast, divorce. What if Lady Audley had another vice, one of which her husband was in the dark? Did her love of horses extend to betting? Had she overindulged in drink and let slip a secret about herself or her husband?

These questions swirled through Dora's mind like wine in a half-empty glass. Each one offered a new path for investigation, but also carried the risk of leading to dead ends. Lord Audley said at the start that there was no need to rush. But the beheaded flowers told a different tale.

Thoughts ricocheted through her mind. Who might it be? What had Lady Audley done? She glanced around the table, searching for inspiration. All she found were reminders of a woman long gone. Lady Audley had entered this house and left her mark, but only Lord Audley's decision not to remarry ensured her memory lived on.

Which begged the question — why now? After twenty-five years of silence, why had someone decided to unearth the past?

Chapter 14
The Grand Plan

After the footman took away the dessert dishes, Lord Audley invited his guests to adjourn to his study for a nightcap. For an hour, they'd set aside their concerns and simply existed in the moment. But with dinner now at a close, it was time to return to business.

Audley's study was his inner sanctum, a place stamped with his presence. Rex inhaled the faint hints of leather and pipe smoke, and remembered the nights he'd spent here on previous missions. He took Lord Audley up on his offer of a snifter of brandy and relaxed into his seat. For a time, no one spoke.

After a lengthy pause, Lord Audley cleared his throat. "I think it is best that you return to your normal behaviour for a time. Your questions have raised eyebrows. Let whoever left this flower believe their warning has been heeded."

Although Audley's suggestion was well-intentioned, Rex was not yet prepared to give up their search. He and Dora had never let fear dictate their movements. They would not start doing so now.

"It is no burden for us to resume our evenings out amongst our set, but surely you cannot mean for us to give up. There was someone at tonight's event who understood the purpose behind our questions about Lady Audley. Should we not request a list of the cocktail reception attendees?"

"I will ask my clerk to get a copy, but I hold little hope it will be of use. You saw how crowded the atrium was. There were over 100 people in attendance, and even more invited. Given the nature of the event, people were constantly coming and going. There will be too many names, with no way to narrow down to a short list. I value you all too much to ask you to waste time. It is smarter to keep your head down and wait for a new clue." Lord Audley sipped from his glass. His heavy gaze stifled Rex's impulse to push back.

Dora suffered from no such restrictions. "What if we change directions instead? We've been so focused on the events of the past, we failed to take into consideration a key question. Why did someone choose to send you this note now, Lord Audley? Do you have any guesses?"

Lord Audley set his glass down and rubbed his forehead. "Do you know, until this moment, I had not given that any consideration? It is a fair point. Unfortunately, I don't have an answer."

Dora refused to let the idea go. "Let us see if we can jog your memory. We three were away for the entire summer. Did you meet someone new? Did you experience any confrontations? Or perhaps settle an old score?"

"No, nothing of the sort. After the royal wedding, I spent some time in the country. Things were quiet in London, and it seemed a good time to get away and clear my head."

Dora tapped her chin. "If it was not something in your life that changed, then it must have been something in the life of whoever sent you the anonymous tip. I cannot imagine it was something small. Whoever it is held their tongue for a quarter of a century. We need to speak to people who were here this summer, and we need to do so in a way that won't arouse suspicion."

"How will you do that?" Lord Audley asked. "Will you go door-to-door, or corner people when they are out at events? Those tactics already caused you trouble."

Dora's eyes slid toward the moustache man sitting across from her. Clark shifted uncomfortably under her gaze.

"Why are you looking at me that way, Theodora?" Clark asked.

"I am recalling a time when we needed access to steal the visitor logs from Whites. It seemed an impossible task, until you came up with a way for us to act in plain sight, with none the wiser."

Rex remembered that night well. He and Dora had despaired of getting into the exclusive London men's club. Then Clark had shown up, and without a moment's hesitation, came up with a foolproof plan to steal the information they'd needed to identify a killer. He had organised an elaborate scavenger hunt, and made the guest book one of the items to find.

Rex was not opposed to dashing around town again, in another madcap escapade, but try as he might, he did not understand how it would help.

"A scavenger hunt?" Clark asked, equally perplexed. "I suppose we can spread ourselves across a few motorcars and speak with a dozen or so people. But how is that any better than circulating around a party?"

"Think bigger," Dora challenged. Even Lord Audley shifted forward to hear more. "I want an event that lasts a full day and night, with every Bright Young Thing in London taking part. As organisers, we will set up checkpoints around town. Everyone involved will be asked to check in throughout the event, to show which items they have found. If we ask them all some variation of the same question, no one will know. And what better to ask than if our event surpasses anything that happened while we were away?"

"You're mad," Lord Audley sighed, but he did not say no.

"Madly brilliant," Clark gasped. His cheeks flushed, and he rubbed his hands together. "It's been quite a while since I last presented a challenge to our set. I do have a certain reputation to uphold, even if I have cleaned up my act."

"Indeed," Dora agreed. "What of you, Rexy darling?"

The thrill of excitement had Rex's blood pumping, but he forced himself to remain levelheaded. "If we do as you suggest, on such a grand scale, it will probably make the papers."

"I will ensure it does," Dora replied, giving him a wink. "Every broadsheet in London will write of our grand adventure — just one more of the crazed antics of our set."

"And with that, none will ever guess the reason you held the event. Although I'm certain the Met will not appreciate me encouraging such misbehaviour, you three have my blessing." Lord Audley rose to top up his glass and asked if anyone else needed a refresh. Rex, Clark, and Dora declined. "What theme will you do?"

"Err, that is a good question." Clark tossed back the last of his drink. "It will take me some time to pull together something on this grand scale."

Rex set his glass aside. Now that everyone was on board, he threw himself in. "There's no need to tax yourself, old chap. We could ask my sister for help. Between all the operas and musicals she has studied, she'll have no trouble coming up with a winning theme."

"I will take help from any source, young Caledonia included. Although, I draw the line in allowing her to be part of the execution of the event."

Rex blanched at the image of his sister riding along with one of the Tennant brothers, or tossing back a drink with the

Mitford sisters. Would she want to take part? Worse yet, would she even listen if he forbade it?

Dora laid a hand on his leg and put him out of his misery. "Caledonia is far too serious a girl to get caught up in such shenanigans. Trust me, helping with the planning and reading about the aftermath in the papers will be enough to satisfy her curiosity."

If they weren't, Rex would assign Caledonia to Clark's motorcar. The threat of another white-knuckle ride through London would certainly be enough to make her think twice.

* * *

The next morning, Rex entered his grandmother's library to find his sister sitting at the large table. Stacks of books and papers covered every inch of the polished wood surface. With her head bent over her work, she reminded Rex of his days spent studying in the Bodleian at Oxford.

"Blimey!" Clark said from behind Rex. "Is this what it takes for you to break Lord Audley's coded messages?"

Caledonia sat up and rubbed her eyes. She seemed somewhat confused when Rex, Clark, and Dora had entered the room. "What? All I need for Lord Audley's messages is a sharpened pencil and a few scraps of paper. Solving them is a matter of brute force in my mind, not from reading books."

Clark grimaced. "That sounds even less appealing. On the days I envy your intelligence, I will bring this scene to mind and remember how little I enjoyed my time studying in the stacks."

Caledonia barked a laugh. "Glad I could help, Lord Clark. Have you come to check my progress? If so, I've only partially good news to report. Come in and I'll tell you about it."

Rex, Clark, and Dora moved deeper into the library. Rex hesitated when he reached the table, not wanting to intrude on his sister's work. If the forgotten half-drunk tea and biscuit crumbs shoved off to the corner of the table were any clue, she'd been at work for hours already. Clark stopped well short of the table and rested his hip on the edge of a small sofa.

Dora suffered from no qualms. She passed Clark and beelined for the table, bending over to read the names printed on the book spines. Caledonia shifted one pile to give her a better view.

"I have made some progress on the third encrypted letter. Before you get too excited, I will add that it reveals nothing of use. Best as I can tell, it is a threat. Lady Audley was to meet the demands or face the consequences."

Rex huffed out a breath, and his shoulders dropped. Given the blackmailer had gone to all the trouble to send encoded messages, the least they could have done was spell things out more clearly. Then again, unsaid words still held meaning. Take the beheaded flowers Dora found in the Rolls the night before.

"I will keep at it for a little while longer. I took a break this morning to give my mind a rest. Now, what brings the three of you here today?"

"This is what rest looks like to you?" Clark threw his hands in the air, as though asking the universe to intervene. "I'm doubly glad we are here. If it is a break you need, this should fit the bill. We'd like your help with planning a scavenger hunt."

Caledonia's head whipped around, excitement lighting her features. "One of your scavenger hunts? The kind that riles up half of London and ends with your photograph in the newspaper?"

"Exactly — only this time, we want to rile all of London and land a special, dedicated section to cover the event. Are you game?"

Caledonia swept her papers together and started

consolidating her stacks. "Am I ever! Push up your sleeves, help me move these books, and I will do all I can."

Rex and Clark did as requested, while Dora rang for refreshments. In short order, the four sat at the table with clean sheets of paper, bone china cups of steaming tea, and a plate of buttered crumpets. While they snacked, Clark explained the criteria for the event.

"This is to be a grand adventure. No prize too great, nor too outlandish. I mean for this hunt to last until midnight and beyond, so we must include plenty of challenges along the way."

"We hoped you could help us with a central theme," Rex added. "Perhaps a musicale or opera?"

Caledonia stared off into space, her gaze going soft. After a few moments, she blinked her eyes and then pushed back her chair. She hurried over to the shelf where they'd put her stacks of books. Her fingers trailed over the spines until she found the one she needed.

"Remember the old diary I found?" Caledonia asked on her way back to the table. "Lady Grace, the writer, lived in London during the Regency period. A little over a century ago," she added.

"So you want us to have a Regency theme?" Clark scrunched his brow, struggling to remember his history. "Who was the regent? Was it Prinny? He was a gas, from what I recall."

"Prinny pales in comparison to his dear mother, Queen Charlotte. She ruled London society with an iron fist wrapped in a silken glove. Our ancestor, Lady Grace, danced like a marionette on strings while Queen Charlotte acted as the puppet master." Caledonia lowered her voice. "Rex, you are not the first member of our family to take an interest in solving crime. It seems you may have inherited your abilities from Grandmama's line."

"That does not surprise me in the least," Dora said. "I am very interested to learn more about Lady Grace, but first, we need to organise the scavenger hunt. Are you proposing we use Queen Charlotte?"

"Indeed, I am. She left her mark on both London and English society. Look here." Caledonia opened the book she'd retrieved and flipped to the section she wanted. "King George bought Buckingham House to be her home, so you can use the palace as one of the stops. Charlotte was an avid gardener, supported scientific thinkers, and welcomed England's most notorious bluestockings to her inner circle. With a little thought, I am certain we can come up with a wide and varied list of treasures to hunt. What do you think?"

Rex looked at Clark. He was the expert on such matters.

Clark took the book from Caledonia and flipped through the pages with a critical eye. Although the man rarely took life seriously, his scavenger hunts were legendary for a reason. He finally closed the book and handed it back. The others at the table held their breaths while waiting for his verdict.

Clark was in his element. He leaned back in his chair and crossed his arms over his chest. Slowly, a smile spread across his face. "Caledonia, you are a genius. I will make sure to give you proper credit when the society columnists come calling."

Caledonia beamed in delight at his initial compliment, but her smile dropped at his last words. "Please, leave my name out of it. The dents that somehow only enhance your reputation won't show nearly as well on mine."

Chapter 15
An Unexpected Recruit

It took a full day of planning to prepare the elaborate scavenger hunt. For once, Clark did not complain, not even when his back twinged after hours spent leaning over the table.

For Dora, the cause evoked the same frisson of excitement she got when planning a spy mission. She telephoned Harris and Inga, requesting they bring themselves and Cynthia to Lady Edith's home at once. Once arrived, Clark and Caledonia split them into teams and gave them an assignment.

Cynthia, Dora's housemaid, took charge of writing invitations to everyone in Clark's social circle. The carefully worded cards provided only enough information to tempt participants to show up at the specified place and time, without giving away any of the game. She worked through the list of names according to where they lived in London. As soon as she finished an area, her brothers, Archie and Basil — also known as Dora's footmen —took charge of their delivery.

Caledonia and Clark spearheaded the hunt itself. Caledonia rattled off suggestions for Clark's consideration. He then weighed the relative ease or difficulty with locating an item in London that would meet the criteria. As he explained to everyone, scavenger hunts required a certain level of challenge, but adding in an impossible find would cause the players to drop out.

To that end, Clark suggested they put a twist on the normal hunt. "We have to give people a reason to stop at the checkpoints throughout the day. What if, instead of me announcing the full list of items at the start, we give them out one at a time?"

"Won't that get annoying after a while?" Inga asked.

"Not if we make the stops part of the game. I am taking a page from our dear Caledonia's book and encrypting the clues. Won't it be interesting to see if anyone shows a particular dexterity at decryption?"

Dora was filled with admiration. "It is a fantastic idea. My only concern is that it might hit too close to the bone."

"Not if we use different forms of encryption," Caledonia said. "And they do not all have to be in an actual code. We can use several puzzle formats to cover up our primary purpose."

Dora glanced at Inga, wanting her thoughts before she spoke up. After all, the two of them had more experience in such matters than anyone else in the room. Inga's brow furrowed and her eyes shifted left and right, but soon enough, she came to a conclusion. She met Dora's gaze and gave a single nod of her head.

"One last question." Dora tapped the watch on her wrist. "Can you get the puzzles made in time?"

"We can if we can have some help," Caledonia replied without missing a beat.

Dora lifted her hand and pointed across the room. "Inga is your girl. Rex and Harris, can you two determine where to set up our checkpoints?"

"We can," Rex answered. He walked across the room, aiming for a stack of paper maps. He searched through until he

Lynn Morrison

found a map of London. "We will look for cafes and pubs near the neighbourhoods relevant to each item. That will give them an additional reason to look forward to the stops."

Dora put her hands on her hips and smiled in delight. "I do so love it when our madcap plans come to fruition. Since you all have everything here under control, I will take my leave."

"And where are you going?" Inga asked, scowling at Dora.

"If we want the gossip rags to cover our antics, someone has to ensure they know about them. I will put a few whispers on the wind right after making sure it is blowing in the right direction."

With that, Dora retrieved her tailored coat, crafted from the finest wool in a rich burgundy, and cinched at the waist with a belt. She stopped in front of a gilded mirror in the front hall to note how it accentuated her silhouette. Her muted gold silk dress peeped out from between her lapels and below the bottom of the knee-length coat.

The butler held out her cloche hat and stood back while she pulled it over her bobbed hair. She glanced down at her T-strap heels, their leather polished to a shine, and decided the heels were too high to make walking practical.

"I hope madam does not mind. I took the liberty of calling for the car," the butler announced.

"I do not mind in the least," Dora assured him. "If I did not value Lady Edith's goodwill as much as I do, I would try to convince you to come work for me."

"I heard that," Harris called from the library doorway. "And what, pray tell, would you have me do?"

Dora fluttered her lashes at her best friend's husband. "Why Harris, I would let you put your feet up and eat bonbons all day. What else did you expect?"

Lady Edith's butler harrumphed at their outrageous

116

behaviour, but Dora caught a twinkle in his eye. With a wave of her hand, Dora set off to accomplish her assignment.

Out of habit, Dora glanced up and down the pavement, surveying her surroundings to keep her skills up to date. The grand facades of the Georgian townhomes lined the streets, their meticulously maintained frontages standing in a silent vigil while their tall windows offered glimpses of the upper class lives inside.

Across the road, lush green boughs stood ready to cast a shade upon Grosvenor Square. Despite the cloudy skies and chill in the air, children danced and played under the watchful eyes of their nannies. Years before, Dora had been one of them. She and her brothers had laughed and squealed while their governess looked on.

And so it was that she had some idea of what type of people to expect walking along the square's paths. In addition to the nannies and children, Dora spied a few servants in grey or black uniforms, no doubt running errands for their households. An elderly woman dressed in clothing more appropriate to the Edwardian years hobbled along, balanced by a wooden cane and the arm of a grandson. The veterans sitting in two chairs, playing chess on a folding table, were new, but not so out of the ordinary as to warrant a second glance.

That left the lone woman. She sat on a wooden bench, her handbag tucked against her side. Her gloved hands held the day's paper wide open. Although it hid her face, it did not cover the fine fabric of her coat, the silk stockings on her legs, nor the Mary Janes Dora had so recently admired in the window of Harrods.

Before she could cross the street to investigate, the Rolls-Royce came to a stop at the kerb. Dora rapped on the driver's window and motioned for him to keep his seat. "Change of plans. I won't be needing the car after all."

Lady Edith's driver tugged his cap down as he nodded his head and then pulled out onto the road to return to the garage in the mews behind the house.

With the way now clear, Dora tucked her clutch under her arm and hurried over to the square as fast as dignity would allow.

She did not bother to disguise her destination. She noted the paper drop by an inch and then the pages flutter. Good. She had managed to disconcert her observer as much as the discovery of her presence had done to Dora.

Dora sauntered over and eased herself onto the bench beside the woman reading the paper. "Nothing interesting today, I'm afraid. Wait until the weekend, and I'm sure Casper Eadmund will have plenty to hash over. Although you'd know better than I do given you write his columns."

Prudence Adams, for it was she, closed her paper with a huff of frustration. "How did you spot me? And how did you know it was me?"

Dora laid a hand on Prudence's arm. "Don't be cross, darling. Rex never would have noticed your presence. I, on the other hand, can spot an expensive pair of shoes at five hundred paces."

Prudence raised her leg high enough to allow them both to admire her new footwear. "They are the bee's knees, are they not?"

"Yes, but if you wanted my opinion on fashion, you had only to ask. Why are you spying on us? Don't bother to deny it — you'll do us both disrespect."

Prudence held her tongue, choosing to fold her paper with care before tucking it under her handbag. Unencumbered, she shifted until she looked Dora straight in the eye.

"I want in."

"On what?"

"Whatever it is you are doing. As you said, don't bother to deny it. The evidence trail is plain as day. First, you asked me to arrange a meeting with Mr Stanley. Then, my uncle mentioned speaking with Rex at an event at Westminster. That is hardly your scene. And now, most of your household is holed up inside the Dowager Duchess's home. You are up to something and I want to be part of it."

Dora found herself in a conundrum. She had, in fact, been on her way to invite Prudence to take part in the scavenger hunt. Now, she feared an easy capitulation would only further arouse the woman's suspicions.

Added to this was that Prudence had been spying on them. Dora had long wondered how Prudence came about the details she cited in her weekly society gossip column. She had assumed Prudence had a network of servants she paid to pass along information from events she did not attend. But the spying opened the door to other options, and those were the ones that intrigued Dora the most.

Right now, Dora had the upper hand, and she intended to make the most of it. However, she would have to walk a careful line if she did not want to reveal more than she intended.

Dora repositioned herself, resting her clutch in her lap and giving every appearance of settling in place for a long conversation.

"Tell me, Prudence, why should we allow you into our inner circle?"

"Am I not already standing on the edge?" Prudence replied. "You were happy enough to manipulate me into helping you in Rome. Turnabout is fair play, is it not?"

"Yes, but there, we had something to offer in trade. We rewarded you handsomely with exclusive information about the identity of the killer of poor Mary. This time, whatever we may or may not be doing shall remain out of the papers."

"If all I wanted was a story, I have enough to make an educated guess. First you ask about an event from ages ago. Then my uncle tells me Rex wanted to discuss Lord Audley's marriage. One trip to the newspaper archives was sufficient for me to confirm you must be looking into Lady Audley's death. I may not know the why, but I am confident I know the what." Prudence crossed her arms over her chest and sat back with a satisfied smile on her face.

Dora did not ease her scrutiny of the other woman. If anything, she sharpened her gaze, raking Prudence from head to toe. Prudence had become accustomed to working undercover. How would she react when placed under the spotlight?

Dora need not have worried. Prudence was made of sterner stuff than the average London society girl. Her breathing did not change under Dora's scrutiny. Her fingers drummed a steady cadence along her crossed arms. Even her cheeks remained free of any telltale blush. Dora was rarely impressed, but even she had to admit Prudence was more than capable.

Dora took a deep breath and released it in a sigh of acceptance. "There will be conditions."

"I would expect no less."

"And a trial period."

"Of course."

"Most importantly," Dora added, lowering her voice so that Prudence had to lean forward. "Do not expect an answer to every single question. This is non-negotiable. Some of the secrets are not ours to share."

Prudence uncrossed her arms and offered Dora her hand. "I accept. Shall we shake on it to finalise our arrangement?"

Dora threw back her head and laughed. "Prudence darling, there are much more enjoyable ways to celebrate a new partnership. If you've nowhere else to be, might I suggest we forgo the traditional handshake in favour of a Champagne toast?"

Prudence arched an eyebrow and tilted her head to the side. "Now? It is not even lunch yet."

Dora remained undaunted. "Are you familiar with Nellie McClung?"

Prudence reared back. "Who?"

"Nellie McClung," Dora repeated. "She is a Canadian suffragette. Commit her name to mind, darling, as I think you'll find her most interesting."

"Sure, but why is she relevant to the matter of drinking before luncheon?"

"Because I choose to live my life as she suggested. *Never retract, never explain, never apologise; get things done and let them howl.*" Dora stood from the bench. "Now, are you going to accept this invitation you so desperately craved, or will you go back to reading your paper?"

Prudence raised her hands to her cheeks and shook her head, in awe of the unapologetic femme fatale known as Theodora Laurent. But soon enough, she grabbed her paper and handbag and rose to her feet. Dora linked their arms and urged Prudence to take the first steps toward changing the rest of her life.

Chapter 16
Carousing with Purpose

Rex had no reason to doubt Dora's judgment. She was intelligent, experienced, and had common sense in spades. But when she snuggled under the covers and announced her intention to train Prudence to become a spy, all those thoughts went out the window.

He rolled over, causing the bed frame to shake, and turned on his table lamp. "Have you lost the plot?" he asked.

Dora blinked against the light. "Do you need the lamp to hear?"

"I need the light to see whether you are lucid. You cannot possibly be serious. Prudence is a-"

"A what?" Dora asked in a husky voice, sharp with the threat of violence. "An upper-class girl?"

"What? No, of course, that is not what I meant. She is a gossip, Dora. How could you ever trust her with your secrets? With any secrets?"

"She has kept her own identity from the world, so she is capable of holding her tongue when properly incentivised."

"She can keep her own secrets. When it comes to everyone

else, she prints them for all the world to see." Rex crossed his arms and refused to lie down.

"How often do you read her columns?"

"Is that relevant?" Rex asked.

"Inga and I pulled a year's worth of them after our return from Rome. Prudence is witty, scathing, but never outright cruel, unless the situation or the individual truly warrants it. Which you'd know if you read her work."

Rex stood strong. "So she has her limits. That makes no difference."

"Yes, it does," Dora countered. She pushed back the covers and sat up. Her delicate hands hid a surprisingly firm grip, which she used to pull Rex's crossed arms apart. "Come now, darling, have a little faith. Intuition tells me that if I can find out why Prudence holds her line, I will know whether we can trust her. If you care to make a wager..."

Rex held up his hands and then pulled his wife into an embrace. He kissed the top of her head, revelling in the clean scent of her reddish-blonde locks. "No wagers. I learned better than to bet against you in our early days. If you believe Prudence is right for the role, carry on. But be forewarned, it is not I that you will ultimately have to convince, but Lord Audley."

Dora lifted her head to nuzzle Rex with her nose. "Leave Lord Audley to me. If I convinced him to take a chance on me, Inga, Harris, you, Cynthia, Archie, Basil, and Clark..."

"You can stop there. I get your point. Goodnight, dear."

Rex slept soundly and awoke with a clear head and can-do attitude. His restful night proved to be a blessing once the scavenger hunt kicked off. He counted more than a dozen cars lined up around Grosvenor Square. Leading the pack was a Rolls-Royce Phantom, its imposing size and elegant lines drawing admiring glances. Although the Rolls was fashionable among the set, it was far from the only motor car of choice. He wished he could take a turn in the white Bentley 3 Litre or the Hispano-Suiza parked behind it. The Bugatti and Alfa Romeo promised speed, but he doubted their drivers' abilities to capitalise on that power on London's busy streets.

It was no wonder the papers referred to this bunch as the bright young things. Their joie de vivre shone for all to see in sparkling smiles, flashy motorcars, and brightly coloured clothing. The styles of their clothing were as varied as their personalities, yet not a one followed the conventions of their parents' generation.

That made it all the more interesting for them to harken back to the Regency days of strict society rules and spotless reputation. In deference to the theme, the women carried silk fans and showcased elaborate hairstyles. The men had followed suit with crisp white cravats tied in elaborate folds Beau Brummell himself would have envied.

Clark stood at the front of the crowd, wearing a coat and breeches like a young buck on his way to Almack's. Based on the smell of mothballs, Rex guessed Clark had sent his servants searching through old trunks in his attic.

Dora, too, had opted for Regency attire. Rex had a newfound respect for women after watching Inga help Dora lace her corset. If the tight garment pained her now, she gave no hint. She strolled along the pavement, distributing sheets of parchment paper with the first set of instructions.

Clark stepped up on a wooden crate and addressed the crowd of participants. "Ladies and Lords of the court of mad King George, you are invited to take part in a grand hunt through our fine city, one which will be like no other. Over the course of the day, you will experience all the main events of the infamous London season. Some of you will rise above your station. Others will fall. Only the brave and adventurous will reach the end."

"Bravery is standing in Grosvenor Square in century-old breeches," a man cried, earning laughs and a smattering of applause.

Clark bowed magnanimously, taking the ribbing in stride, and then wagged a finger at the man. "Say that again and it will be pistols at dawn, Beaton."

Cecil Beaton handed his ever-present camera to a friend and pretended to stumble and fall from his wound. Dora burst into loud sobs and rushed to his side, playing the hysterical young love to perfection. The crowd lapped up their antics, just as Clark had intended.

Rex would never have the gumption to do what Clark did, nor Dora, for that matter. That was the benefit of being part of a team. Everyone contributed something unique to forge a stronger whole.

Clark coughed to get everyone's attention and continued. "For each stage of this hunt, you will have an item to find and a place to deliver it. We, the organisers, will tell you each item, but to find out where to deliver it, you will have to decipher a clue. You have in your hands your first challenge. Theodora, will you be a darling and read it for the group?"

"Mais, oui!" Dora sauntered back to the front of the group and took Clark's place on the wooden crate. "It is an excerpt from a poem—"

"And, by frequenting sacred groves, grew wise.
Free from the impediments of light and noise,
Man, thus retired, his nobler thoughts employs.
Here Charles contrives the ordering of his states,
Here he resolves his neighbouring princes' fates;"

"Blimey," a woman groaned, putting a hand to her brow. "Now I wish I had paid more attention during my lessons."

A group of Oxford boys down for the summer looked fit to burst and immediately heckled the poor girl.

Clark waved his hands to quiet the crowd. "Figure out what the poem's lines represent and you will know where to go. If you need help, it will come at a cost. Interpret the clue or impress us with your waltzing skills. Either way, Miss Laurent and I will depart in our carriage in exactly ten minutes."

With a last flourish, Clark raised his pocket watch high. "Meet us there with an old-fashioned debutante's locket. On your mark, get set, go!"

What happened next can only be described as utter pandemonium. The teams, divided by motorcar, clustered in groups along the pavement edging Grosvenor Square. Some shouted and argued, others whispered. The Oxonians leapt into their car and drove off. Their departure lit a fire under the remaining.

Clark and Dora hummed the tune of a waltz for those who chose to dance rather than fall behind. One by one, the teams took off, hunting for the item. When the last left, Rex climbed into his Rolls and started the engine. Clark and Dora joined him, and together they set off on a sedate drive.

As to their destination, where else could the season start but with a presentation to the queen? In her pale green silk gown, white gloves, and pearls, Dora was sure to be named a diamond of the first water. With that in mind, the trio headed for Queen Charlotte's London home — Buckingham House. A century earlier, Buckingham House had been one of London's fine homes, only later, under her son's guidance, undergoing the transformation into the grandiose palace of today.

Of course, taking the hunt into the palace itself was out of the question. Instead, Inga, Prudence, and Harris awaited them on the lawn of St James's Park, on the corner nearest the palace gates. They had spread picnic blankets across the grass and set out tables of cakes and punch.

Despite the organised, if somewhat unruly, start, the event soon disintegrated into the chaos their set of friends adored. Rex, Dora, and the others ended up spread across London, some staying a step ahead of the leaders, while others remained behind to cheer on the stragglers.

The true test was arriving at 43 Club after midnight with every single participant in tow. The revellers celebrated their accomplishments with champagne bottles and flasks of gin and whiskey while dancing until the wee hours of the next morning.

They hardly noticed Rex, Dora, Clark, and Prudence sneak away. The foursome fought back exhaustion for long enough to make it safely home. They dropped Clark at his house with the promise to regroup over a full English breakfast. As for Prudence, she stayed the night in Dora's guest room.

The next morning dawned far too early. Rex begged Archie to leave the pot of coffee on the table rather than to pour him a single cup. Dora sailed into the room, looking none the worse for wear despite the late night.

"Swap the coffee for Inga's famous hangover cure," she suggested, earning a groan of disgust from Rex.

"No, please, not that. Coffee will do me just fine. I am exhausted, not suffering from overindulgence." To emphasise his point, Rex raised his cup for a top-up.

It was only then that he noticed he was drinking from a Chinoiserie teacup instead of his normal mug. He glanced around the dining room, noting the stack of hand-painted porcelain plates sitting atop the dining hutch. Plants of various sizes sat on the windowsill overlooking the garden. The pièce de résistance was the silver tiara sitting atop a marble bust Rex had brought back from Rome.

In the madcap events of the day before, he had given no

Lynn Morrison

thought to what Archie and Basil were doing with the scavenger hunt finds. He suspected Harris was behind the decision to incorporate the random bits and bobs into the decor of Dora's home.

The man himself entered the room next, guiding both Prudence and Clark to the table. Harris held out the chair for Prudence to sit while Archie poured coffee and juice. Basil followed with plates of steaming breakfast straight from the kitchen.

Dora invited Harris to join them, and Inga followed suit. The hot breakfast of blood sausage, beans, roasted tomatoes, mushrooms, and toast revived them all better than any medical tonic. Twenty minutes later, in a much better frame of mind, the group adjourned to the drawing room.

"I call this meeting of the minds to order," Dora said. "Our aim yesterday was two-fold. First, to provide a distraction to anyone attempting to follow our investigation into Lady Audley's death. Second, to learn what we could about anything unusual which happened this summer while we were all abroad. Prudence, we will begin with you."

As part of the conditions for her participation, Prudence had shared her pseudonym with everyone and promised to cover the scavenger hunt in the society pages.

"I spoke with Mr Sanderson at the Sunday Pictorial several times yesterday. His photographer got plenty of shots to use in the weekend edition. I'll type my column today and have it sent round for publication."

Dora rewarded her with a smile. "Excellent. Then, let us proceed to point two. I heard tell of two broken engagements, one torrid affair, and several people who lost their shirts playing cards."

"That's all in a day's work for our set," Clark grumbled. "I didn't do much better. I asked around about people's parents

128

and got nothing other than wrinkled noses and strange looks. Can't say I blame them. Who wants to have a chinwag about old people?"

"Do not let Lord Audley hear you say that," Rex warned. "I also came up short. Harris, Inga, did either of you have luck?"

Harris and Inga shook their heads. Rex covered his face with his hands and groaned. All that effort, and they had nothing other than some newsprint to show for it.

"Fear not, Rex," Inga said, breaking into his doldrums. "When you and the others left for the 43 Club, I had a look at the results for the various stages of the hunt. One team consistently outdid the rest when it came to solving the riddles. They would have won the challenge if not for their unwillingness to enter a women's shop to get a tiara."

Rex lowered his hands and sat up straight. Inga would not mention this if it weren't relevant.

"The Oxford boys, down for the summer, solved every riddle in record time, including the one Caledonia designed to mimic Lady Audley's letters."

"Down for the summer.... Could that be the thing that changed?" Dora urged Inga to spill the rest of what she knew.

"I do believe that it is. For, amongst the names I overheard the boys use, one stuck out."

"Ketchum," Harris blurted, stealing his wife's thunder. He jerked to the side before Inga whacked him with the roll of papers in her hands. "Sorry, dear. I got caught up in the excitement."

Inga's glare promised retribution. She turned back to the group and wiggled her brow. "What do you think is the likelihood that this Ketchum is related to Lord and Lady Ketchum?

"So which one is it?" Prudence asked, shifting in her seat with excitement.

"Both were at the Wiltshire Ball. Both might have been at the Westminster event; we will have to check the guest list to see." Dora tapped her fingers on the armrest of her chair. "Did Lady Ketchum uncover some sort of an illicit arrangement between her husband and Lady Audley? Or was Lord Ketchum the one making the threats? We can hardly go to them now and ask. They'd laugh us out of the room."

Rex could see only one way forward. "We will have to investigate them both, looking into their past and their present. Any suggestions of where to start?"

"We will split again into teams," Dora replied. "Women on Lady Ketchum, and you men on his lordship. Find out as much as you can, and we will regroup at dinner."

Chapter 17
Blooming with Problems

Dora and Prudence took turns making telephone calls to prepare for their research. First, Prudence rang Mr Stanley to ask whether he would be willing to tell them more about Lord and Lady Ketchum. He agreed and invited them to come round in the early afternoon.

Prudence then took advantage of the remainder of the morning to prepare her society column for submission. Dora rang Lady Edith and her mother in that order. She asked them whether they had any insight into Lord and Lady Ketchum's marriage. She received a similar answer from both: the Ketchum's marriage was rather unremarkable. It bore neither the hallmarks of a deep, abiding love, nor those of a contentious relationship. Like so many other marriages within the upper class, Lord and Lady Ketchum had found a way to coexist, but little more.

Dora was not sure what to do with that information. It would have been simpler if one of the Ketchums had a reputation for cruelty or emotional outbursts. However, the more she reasoned, the more she realised why that would not be the case. Whoever had committed the crime of blackmailing

Lady Audley had got away with it for twenty-five long years. It would take a cold-blooded individual to keep that a secret for such a long time.

Of course, that raised the question again of why now. Assuming that it was either Lord or Lady Ketchum who had sent the notes to Lady Audley, why had their son's return from school this summer led to someone revealing the information? Dora found a piece of paper and made a note to herself to look more into the son after they finished their investigations into the parents.

Prudence finished her column in short order, and Dora asked Archie to carry it to the paper. The women sat down for a short luncheon of bread, cheeses, and cold meats, neither in the mood for anything heavier. When they finished, Basil brought the car around to drive them over to Bloomsbury.

The women used the ride over to agree on what they would and would not tell Mr Stanley. The man had a veritable treasure trove of information, and he knew it. There was little chance he would answer their questions without extracting something in return. It fell to Dora to make the final decision.

"We might as well tell him we are looking into the death of Lady Audley, but only if he agrees not to tell anyone else. He strikes me as the type of man who appreciates holding information in confidence," Dora said.

"Yes, especially now that he is retired," Prudence agreed. "Are you certain that Lord Audley will not mind that we shared this with Mr Stanley?"

"Do not worry. I will tell him it slipped out in an unguarded moment. What could I do? It is not as though I could take it back once the words left my mouth." Dora shrugged her shoulders, causing Prudence to laugh.

The streets around Bloomsbury teemed with motorcars and delivery lorries. Dora instructed Basil to let them off where they were. They were close enough to arrive faster if they completed the rest of their journey on foot. The women struck out along the pavement, drawing plenty of eyes.

For once, Prudence was attracting a fair amount of attention. Dora was dressed in the latest fashion of wide-leg trousers in a bold print and a cloche, as she always was. Since Prudence had chosen more sedate clothing, everyone stared at her in curiosity, wondering how she had become friends with such an elegant woman.

Dora was certain that no one had guessed the truth. She entertained herself by watching the reflections of passersby in the windows of the shops. Caught up as she was in studying people's expressions, it took her several minutes to realise that someone was following them.

It was a man, or at least someone dressed like a man. With his hat pulled low and the collar of his jacket flipped up, he stayed far enough back that Dora could not get a good look at his face. She supposed it could be a coincidence that he was walking in the same direction, but his outfit and mannerisms made her suspicious. She did not, however, say anything about him to Prudence.

Mr Stanley answered his door at the first press of the buzzer. He welcomed the women into his home once again and invited them to take seats in his sitting room. He had already searched through his notes to find information on the Ketchums, Prudence having alerted him to the reason for their visit. As expected, he balked at answering any questions until they explained why they were asking. His eyebrows crept up his forehead, and his eyes grew wide when Dora explained they were working on Lord Audley's behalf.

"I have long thought that there are hidden depths to Lord Audley's character and behaviour, but I assumed his interests were purely political. I remember his wife well and was saddened by her death. If someone was responsible for her early demise, they should be held accountable. Please, ask me anything you want, if you think it will help," he offered.

"Thank you," Dora replied. "I will leave it to you to decide whether you want us to share word of your generosity with Lord Audley, or if you prefer to keep your assistance a secret."

"Oh, a secret for sure," Mr Stanley laughed and waved his hands. "I am certain that Lord Audley does not know who I am, and I would prefer to keep it that way."

With an agreement in place, Mr Stanley opened his files. "How much do you know about the so-called 'dollar princesses'?"

Dora knew a fair amount, given most considered her mother to be one. However, she could hardly reveal that to her present company. "I am not familiar with the term," she said, layering on her French accent.

"In the latter part of Queen Victoria's reign, the British aristocracy found itself in an unfortunate position. To put it plainly, many of our nation's most highly placed families were short of funds. The ever-enterprising Americans saw an opportunity to change everyone's fortunes. Wealthy American families sent their marriageable-aged daughters to take part in the British season, in the hopes they would catch the eye of titled young men."

"I had always wondered about the sudden influx of Americans," Prudence said. "What I don't understand is how they gained entrée to society. Even the most British of girls could have found herself turned away if her family's reputation was not up to snuff."

"Haven't you learned by now that money can open all doors?" Mr Stanley replied. "So it was back then. Widows and spinsters in need of funds offered to sponsor the Americans in exchange for a small fee, which the Americans were happy to pay."

"I take it Lady Ketchum was one of these so-called dollar princesses," Dora said.

"Indeed, she was, and hardly the first or the last. Until you two came knocking at my door, I would have rated her marriage as one of the better ones."

"Really?" Prudence arched an eyebrow. "We had not heard that the couple were particularly affectionate."

"They were not, but for that generation of women, the definition of success looked quite different," he noted. "Take the Duke and Duchess of Dorset. Their love match was a rare exception. Of course, the Duke of Dorset was flush in the pocket and had the liberty to marry for love. At the opposite end, the Duke of Marlborough married Consuelo Vanderbilt to save Blenheim Palace, and in doing so, ruined their lives for a long while."

"Until they eventually divorced," Dora said. "I ran into Consuelo in Paris, and she is completely enamoured with Jacques Balsan, as is he with her—a very dashing gentleman, I might add."

Prudence took in the information with great interest. She seemed as captivated by the tales as desiring to solve the mystery of Lady Audley. "Why do you think so many of the dollar princess marriages ended in unhappiness, especially given how eager the American girls were to marry into the aristocracy?"

Mr Stanley shifted forward, pleased to have his protégé seek his opinion once more. "I am not sure how many of the American women had a choice in the matter. Take Consuelo Vanderbilt for a moment. Her mother was the force behind her wedding, as she sought the pedigree associated with a title. For all of America's freedoms and democracy, some wished to live like kings. The dollar princesses arrived here without a solid understanding of what it meant to have an upperclass marriage. They expected storybook endings and were met with the harsh slap of reality. To make matters worse, the British women hardly rolled out the red carpet. They resented the outsiders for stealing their suitors."

"That is an uncomfortable position," Dora agreed. When Prudence and Mr Stanley glanced her way, she explained, "I have felt the burn of plenty a cold shoulder here in London, and in other places. Why do you think I move around so much? If it weren't for Lady Edith embracing my relationship with dear Rex, I would be sitting in another city by now."

Prudence reached over and grasped Dora's hand. "That treatment is not limited to foreigners. Without my tragic backstory, I am certain I would not be welcome everywhere I am. With it, I more often feel like an oddity on display rather than a guest."

"Is that why you decided to pick up the proverbial pen?"

Prudence gave a shrug of her shoulders. "In part. I know just how golden the lives are seen as, but how thin the layer of gilt is across the top. The rich have so much and do so little for society as a whole. Someone has to hold them accountable. Why not me? That's why my column looks slightly different from Mr Stanley's, no offence intended," she added.

Mr Stanley took the hit on the chin. "None taken, my dear. We each have to find our unique angle."

"Indeed. I chose not to write about dresses and who snuck away with who. I subtly encourage people to do better by rewarding those who do. Above all else, I want to make the upper class seem as human as the rest of us. With their foibles on display, perhaps fewer will idolise them. To be sure, there is little there to admire with most. You, Lord Rex, and Lord Clark are rare exceptions."

Dora took care to make her resulting smile appear grateful rather than cat-like. Prudence was proving to be an excellent recruit to the spy trade, even if she had yet to learn of it. Feigning respect and interest in leaders was as much a required skill as remembering deep in your heart that they were no better than anyone else.

After clearing her throat, Dora returned the conversation to their original topic. "What of Lady Ketchum's marriage?"

"A financial matter, to be sure," Mr Stanley said. "Previous generations of the Ketchum family had proved to be incapable of managing their finances. When the current Lord Ketchum entered into the marriage mart, there was little doubt he would need to marry a wealthy heiress, although few expected him to wed an American. Most believe their fathers arranged it. If so, it was a shame. The old Lord Ketchum had little time to enjoy the fruits of his daughter-in-law's bank balance, as he died a year after their marriage."

"What of the Wiltshire Ball? The notes you gave us during our last visit mentioned Lord and Lady Ketchum together. Why was that of interest to you?"

"Because they had a row. They rarely engaged in any sort of public displays of emotion, affection or otherwise. For the most part, they arrived at society events together, but soon went their separate ways. Lady Ketchum had a small group of friends, most American. Lord Ketchum would retreat to the card room."

"Did you ever figure out what led to their argument?"

"Not that I can recall, nor could I find in my notes. Most of the mentions I had of Lady Ketchum came from prior to her marriage." To prove his point, Mr Stanley passed his old paper cards to Dora and Prudence.

Dora was not ready to admit defeat. "I heard from a reliable source that Lady Audley had offered Lady Ketchum an olive branch that evening and introduced Lady Ketchum to some of her acquaintances. Would Lord Ketchum have done anything to smooth society's acceptance of his wife?"

Mr Stanley gave Dora's question consideration but eventually shook his head. "No, I cannot imagine he would, and certainly not after the wedding. By then, he had what he needed from Lady Ketchum — well, short of an heir, which she subsequently provided."

Prudence raised a finger. "We believe one of them had something to do with Lady Audley's death. If not Lord Ketchum, what of Lady Ketchum? She married a veritable stranger to gain a title, caring little that he chose her in order to save his estate. Would she have done something else to improve their fortunes?"

"To that, I have no answer. Of the pair, Lord Ketchum always struck me as the one more eager to see and be seen. But that does not prevent the possibility of Lady Ketchum giving him direction from behind the curtain. Certainly, the Ketchum family fortunes changed when she joined them."

With that, Dora and Prudence were once again no further ahead than they had started. They skimmed over Mr Stanley's notes, and jotted down anything that might prove useful, precious little as there was. Then they thanked him for his hospitality and said they would be on their way.

Before they left, Dora moved closer to the window and glanced outside. Their follower stood in a doorway a few doors down, smoking a cigarette. He had lowered his collar, but stood with his head turned away. Although she still could not see his face, she was unsurprised to note he had brown hair. So, too, had the man who had bumped into Rex at the Westminster event.

Dora weighed her options. She could march downstairs and hurry over to confront him. However, he was far enough away to make a run for it before she could reach him. Dressed as she was, and in the company of Prudence and Mr Stanley, climbing on the roof or any of her other tricks were out of the question.

That did not mean she was going to sit back and let whoever this was get away with following her. It was time to do something about him, but doing so would require a hand.

Dora turned around and asked Mr Stanley if she could borrow his telephone. With his permission, she stepped into his hallway and lifted the handset. When the operator came on the line, she gave her home number. Inga answered after a few rings.

"Hello, darling! Prudence and I are having a wonderful adventure. Would you mind terribly if we extended our outing to include a brief shopping trip? I need to pick up a gift for a friend."

Inga immediately understood the subtext of the question. Dora had someone on her tail and needed help to catch them.

"I saw some nice handbags at Selfridges. You should check there."

"I will, indeed. Thanks for the tip, darling. You always know just what I need. I will keep an eye out for a little something for you, too."

"Don't search too hard. I am sure the perfect gift will have a way of making itself known."

With that, Dora rang off. She returned to the parlour, thanked Mr Stanley again, and left. Outside, she latched arms with Prudence. "I hope you aren't in a rush, as we need to make another stop before returning home."

"My time is yours," Prudence replied. "Especially if this stop has anything to do with the mysterious chap who is following us."

Chapter 18
Shopping for More Than a Handbag

R ex and Clark returned home in the early afternoon with downcast expressions on their faces and empty hands. Their trip to the Houses of Parliament had failed to turn up anything useful. Thus, they came inside, went straight to the drawing room, and flopped into their chairs.

Inga, who had witnessed their arrival, asked, "No luck, I take it?"

Rex raised his hands and scrubbed his face. "No smoking gun, no bloody knife, nothing of interest at all. Lord Ketchum's time in the House of Lords can only be described as unremarkable."

"Is it possible that is by choice?" Inga asked.

"Clark, you are the expert here on parliamentary matters," Rex said, passing the ball to Clark.

"Anything is possible, but I don't believe that is the case. You two are accustomed to dealing with Lord Audley, a man of great power and intellect. I suppose I set a counterpoint to his example. Until recently, I only turned up when I had nothing else better to do with my time. Lord Ketchum sits in neither of those camps. His attendance record is exemplary, and over the course of his tenure, he has sat upon several important committees. However, he has yet to sit as the lead on anything. His sphere of influence ensures him a place in the room, but nothing beyond that. The problem is that I cannot see how knowing this helps us build a case against him."

Inga drummed her fingers on the armrest of her wingback chair. After a moment of thinking, she asked, "What if Lord Ketchum rose no higher because Lady Audley died?"

"What do you mean?" Clark asked.

"Well, if he were the one sending her the coded letters, perhaps it was because he wanted her to sponsor him, for lack of a better term, in her conversations with her husband. Lord Audley's backing has changed the future of many a man, present company included."

Clark and Rex exchanged glances, each looking to the other for an opinion on Inga's statement. The trill of the telephone interrupted their conversation. Inga said she would answer it and hurried into the hallway to where the telephone sat.

Deep in thought, Rex paid little attention to Inga's conversation. The call was brief, and Inga soon returned to the room.

"That was Theodora. It seems she has picked up a follower. She is going to lead them to Selfridge's on Oxford Street, hoping the two of you will catch and identify the man. You had best leave now if you want to be there."

"Is Prudence still with her?" Clark asked.

"Yes, they are together. They will walk over from Bloomsbury to give you time to get into place. And you need not worry on their behalf. Theodora knows how to take care of herself."

Rex leapt to his feet before Clark could ask any other questions. Now was not the time to provide an explanation about Dora's self-defence skills, nor how she acquired them.

"Ask Harris to bring around the car. He can drop us off and then come in to help after he has parked the car somewhere nearby."

For once, London's traffic played nicely. With Harris at the wheel, the Rolls-Royce sped up the eastern edge of Hyde Park and soon arrived at Nash's Marble Arch. Harris pulled over to let the men out there, since Selfridge's was only a short walk away along Oxford Street.

Selfridge's grand facade greeted Rex and Clark with its imposing presence on a prominent corner. The grand windows promised an array of luxurious goods inside. The interior was equally impressive, with elaborate displays, a wide variety of departments, and attentive service that made shopping an experience rather than a chore. The handbag department, where Rex and Clark found themselves, was no exception, showcasing the latest in fashion and design.

Rex and Clark scanned their surroundings, checking for any sign of Dora or Prudence. However, there was no woman there with Dora's distinct hair colour. The men decided that they had arrived first.

"We can hardly mill around here, Rex. We stand out like sore thumbs," Clark said.

Rex motioned for Clark to follow him. They wove between the tables full of evening bags and wallets, past the display counters where women in starched uniforms stood ready to help. They came to a stop on the edge of the men's shoe department.

"How is the view from here?" Rex asked, turning to Clark, who stood a few inches taller. Clark bobbed left and right, checking the various angles.

"The perfume display is blocking my view. I can only see the edge of the handbag department nearest the front entrance."

"Well, that will have to be enough. When Theodora and Prudence arrive, we'll move closer."

The men pretended to peruse the shoes for what felt like forever, but was likely only a few minutes. Clark picked up one pair and then another, giving every appearance of being a serious shopper. He offered a shoe to Rex, as though asking for his opinion, and whispered, "How will we know when they arrive? We cannot exactly stare at the doors."

"Oh, we'll know," Rex assured his friend. It was not boasting so much as a hard-earned confidence. By now, Rex had watched Dora enter rooms of all sizes and places, with kings and queens in the audience all the way down to pretending to be a scullery maid. Unless Dora took great care to hide her shine, people noticed. Rex was not immune, either. She had only to enter their bedroom and close the door behind her to get his desires rising.

But for all that Rex had seen and done with Dora, he had never accompanied her on a shopping trip. In fact, until that moment, he had prided himself on steering clear of a long day spent carrying her mountains of purchases. When Dora wanted to go, either Inga or Harris were happy to accompany her.

And so, Rex was wholly unprepared for the shop clerks' reactions to the arrival of the famed Theodora Laurent.

The ripple of whispers began the moment Dora set foot through the door. The clerk at the front make-up counter waved over one of the perfume ladies. She scurried over to the next nearest clerk, and so it went on down the line.

Even from where Rex stood, he could hear shoppers talking, some asking who Dora was, while others filled them in. Dora and Prudence did not get far before a savvy clerk swooped in to help them. Rex shifted closer, curious to hear what would happen next.

"Miss Laurent, what a pleasure it is to have you with us today. Can I show you something specific?" The clerk, a young woman of similar age to Dora and Prudence, wrapped an arm around Dora to direct her to the staircase. "Perhaps you would be interested in our new selection of fur coats? Winter will be upon us soon enough."

To her credit, Dora stood firm. "In truth, I came in search of a handbag."

The older woman standing at the edge of the handbag section gasped in delight. "Miss Laurent, over here! Have you seen the newest evening bags from Coco Chanel?"

"I can never say no to a fellow Frenchwoman," Dora agreed. "In fact, I was telling my cher amie here, Miss Prudence Adams, about how much you have to offer here. Wasn't I, Prudence?"

Prudence stood with the wide-eyed expression of a doe facing a line of hunters. She bobbed her head, but Rex doubted she knew to what she was agreeing.

The original clerk was not about to let the possibility of a large commission slip from her grasp. She scooted between Dora and the handbags. "The handbags are indeed lovely, but would it not make sense to first peruse our selection of evening gowns and day dresses? Clothing first, then shoes, and finally a new bag to top off the look. You should come along as well, Miss Adams. Any connection to Lord Adams?"

Again, Prudence nodded her head, although her complexion had paled considerably in the face of so much attention. Between the shop girls and the customers, the crowd surrounding her and Dora was growing larger by the moment.

It was that thought that spurred Rex to remember why they were there. He spun around to look for Clark and found his friend still holding a black leather dress shoe.

"Come on," Rex murmured, waving Clark forward.

Clark jerked into action and hurried to approach the main entrance, where they would hopefully figure out who had followed Dora there. In his haste, he forgot to put down the shoe in his hand.

"Sir, sir!" a man called from behind. The uniformed shop clerk bustled after Clark. "The shoe, sir. You cannot carry it around."

Rex did not slap his hand over his face, but it was a near thing. He waved his hands at Clark to stop him and pointed at the shoe.

Clark spun around, his face already flushing red in embarrassment. "I am ever so sorry, good man," he muttered loud enough for Rex to hear.

The clerk's stern expression caused Rex to feel a twinge of worry for his friend. Torn as he was between watching the front entrance and helping Clark, he decided it would be fastest to settle matters with the clerk rather than having the man chasing them around the store.

"We'll take two pairs," Rex said. "Size nine, and wrap them for us, please."

The clerk stumbled to a halt at Rex's voice and twisted to see him instead of Clark. That was when Rex learned his face had become as famous as his paramour.

"Lord Rex! Did you accompany Miss Laurent today? How did we miss you coming in?" The clerk opened his arms wide. "Those shoes are hardly appropriate for a man of your standing. Please, allow me to show you our exclusive collection, direct from Italy."

"But we can't right now," Clark blurted.

"Wait, you are Lord Clark Kenworthy! Oh, is this another one of your scavenger hunts? Am I going to be in the newspapers? Where are the photographers?" The male clerk smoothed the lapels of his coat before motioning for one of his coworkers to join them. "Run upstairs to the head office and let them know Lord Clark Kenworthy and Lord Reginald Bankes-Fernsby are here as well."

Clark grabbed a hold of Rex's arm and muttered an apology.

145

His little mistake was quickly blooming into a gigantic problem. There was no hope of them hiding their presence in Selfridges. If the man following Dora had not turned tail and run yet, he certainly would soon.

Still, Rex was not ready to give up. He spun around and scooted from one side to the other, checking the front entrance for any sign of suspicious characters. Unfortunately, the only person he saw acting strangely was Harris. Dora's trusty butler lurked near the front door, doing his best to keep a low profile. He stood out for the simple fact that he was the only person on the ground floor not flocking to take a gander at Dora.

It took Rex, Clark, Dora, and Prudence a full hour to extricate themselves from the determined clutches of the Selfridges staff. Rex did his best to forget how much he had spent, simply to speed things along. At least Clark and Dora seemed happy enough with their purchases.

With Prudence's assistance, Rex convinced Dora and Clark it was time to go. Harris had the motorcar waiting outside when they emerged, blinking against the bright sunlight after so much time inside. Clark sat in the front seat next to Harris, needing the extra room to hold his packages. Prudence ended up with a hatbox in her lap, while Rex found himself half-buried under hanging bags. Dora spent the drive reapplying her lipstick.

Inga greeted them as soon as they came in the door. She hardly arched an eyebrow at the signs of the expenditures, as accustomed as she was to Dora's shopping habits. "Please tell me you got more than some new clothing," she begged. "A name? A look at the man's face?"

"The only names I got were from the various clerks rushing to do our bidding. Once they recognised us all, we did not have a moment to ourselves."

Inga took the news on the chin. "Fear not, I suspect whoever it was will be back. Now that we are forewarned, we can be in position to catch them from the get go. Oh, Rex — something came for you while you were out." Inga picked up an envelope from the side table in the hall.

Rex did not recognise the handwriting on the front. He took care to tear the envelope without ripping the paper inside. It was a single sheet, much wrinkled, and covered in a few lines of jumbled text.

"Is that what I think it is?" Dora asked, scooting closer to him.

"A coded message... or I should say, a new coded message. Harris?" Rex called. He glanced back at the door where Harris still stood with his coat and hat on. "Could you run this over to our cryptologist?"

"Straight away," Harris replied. "I will ask them to ring as soon as they determine what it says."

With that, Harris rushed out the front door to the motorcar parked out front. Dora took the envelope from Rex's hand and examined its appearance. "I don't recognise the handwriting. Do you?"

Rex shook his head. "I wish I did. But even if we cannot put a name to it, there is one thing we can do."

Dora completed his thought. "We can compare it to the handwriting on the note Lord Audley received that started all of this off."

Chapter 19
A Meeting of the Minds

The investigation ground to a halt while everyone waited for Caledonia to decipher the remaining messages. For the most part, the group returned to their normal lives. Prudence returned to her uncle's London manse. Clark put in an appearance in the dining hall of the House of Lords, acting as jovial as ever. Dora joined Benedict for some sightseeing with her visiting cousin (even if said cousin remained unaware of their true connection).

Rex was the only one who continued their research. He took the train to Oxford to find out what he could of the Ketchums' son, explaining to those he met that the young Lord Felix had applied for a government position. Felix had a reputation for doing exactly enough as was needed to pass his exams, and little more. His tutors expressed frustration over his lack of dedication to anything beyond embroiling himself in the shenanigans of the Bullingdon Club. The young man delighted in sowing the seeds of chaos wherever he trod.

While interesting, that knowledge did little to explain how he might be involved in someone's decision to send Lord Audley the message about his wife.

That did not stop Dora from examining all the possibilities. Early one morning, while the rest of upper class London slumbered in their beds, she and Inga tucked themselves away in Dora's private study. Accessible only via a door hidden behind a bookshelf in the library, the study was the rare space where Dora felt comfortable letting her hair down and simply being herself.

Thus, the women did not bother with getting ready for the day.

Inga wore a full-length nightgown made of silk, with fine lace around the collar and cuffs. Her robe was of the same material, in a flattering shade of pale blue. Her auburn hair hung loose, with a delicate hairpin keeping it out of her face. In stark contrast, Dora's bold, red silk gown featured a low neckline and a daring slit up the side. The kimono, cinched at her waist with a matching red sash, protected her modesty. Her golden blonde locks curled around her face.

They carried cups of coffee into the room and took full advantage of the comfortable seating. It was only once they were settled that Dora realised how long it had been since they had last spent time on their own. Over the past year, their household had expanded to include husbands, servants, an ever-widening circle of friends, and one ever-present cat. The only reason Mews wasn't with them then was because Dora had shooed him away from the door.

"I've missed this," Inga said, echoing Dora's private thoughts. "I would not trade Harris and Rex away for all the money in the world, but it is nice to sometimes be on our own."

"I wholeheartedly agree," Dora replied. She took a sip of her coffee and allowed her mind to drift into the past. She and Inga had struck up their friendship in the most difficult of circumstances. They had clung tight to one another, anchoring themselves against the storm of working on the front lines. Entering into the spy service had been almost a lark.

For half a decade, the women had been content to let life lead them wherever it wanted. By shared agreement, they would continue to do so. Both fully enjoyed the freedom and excitement that came along with the responsibility of spying on behalf of England.

But someday, undoubtedly in the far distant future, the women would grow old and have to settle down. Dora tried to imagine herself dolled up in a glittering gown while walking with a cane.

"What thought has got your face so screwed up?" Inga asked.

Dora told her. Inga's eyes crossed as she tried to picture the scene, and she soon erupted into laughter.

Dora set her cup down and crossed her arms over her chest. "Why is that so funny to you? Do you think me incapable of charming information out of foreign leaders when I am no longer young and attractive?"

"Nothing of the sort," Inga answered, once she got herself under control. "Rather, I find it hilarious that you opted to age up your current persona rather than opting for something more akin to the stately and wise Lady Edith. But if you want to sashay into your eighties, who am I to judge?"

Inga was correct, but Dora was just contrary enough to not want to admit it. "I am willing to bet Edith is more spritely than you think. Next time we are all together, I am going to see if I can convince her to dance a jig. Then we will see who is right."

Inga opened her arms wide and welcomed the challenge. After all, either way, she was in for an entertaining experience. "I will look forward to such an event with bated breath. Unless you have some other ridiculous challenge to issue, might I suggest we turn our intelligence toward a more pressing problem? Shall we review our suspects?"

Despite being in housecoats, the pair were nothing if not methodical. They wrote each suspect's name on a separate scrap of paper and then laid them across the low table in front of the sofa.

Dora lifted the first piece of paper from the line, held it up, and read the name aloud. "Lady Ketchum. What are the arguments for and against her being Lady Audley's blackmailer?"

"Lady Ketchum said Lady Audley went out of her way to befriend her, and introduced her to others within her circle. Prior to that, Lady Ketchum had few friends among the aristocracy. If she were desperate enough, she might have used whatever information was available to gain entrée to the right people." Inga gathered her thoughts before continuing, "Alternatively, you said Lady Ketchum seemed genuinely distraught that day at your mother's home."

"Although the expression only briefly flashed across her face, in my expert opinion, it was sadness and not guilt." Dora set the paper with Lady Ketchum's name down and picked up the next one. "That brings us to Lord Ketchum. I must admit I am leaning his way, but that is only because I am sympathetic to his wife. Of course, that is likely because she somewhat reminds me of my mother, so I am hesitant to put too much faith in my gut."

"Then allow me to be the impartial one. We know that Lord Ketchum argued with his wife in the garden on the night of the Wiltshire ball. What if he did so to provide himself with an excuse in case he was seen wandering alone?"

"While your logic holds up, I would be remiss if I did not point out that the same rationale applies equally well to Lady

Ketchum," Dora said with a frown on her face. "Do we have anything else to suggest it was him?"

Inga shook her head.

"That leaves us with their son, Lord Felix. The only thing we know for certain is that he cannot be our blackmailer, because he wasn't alive back then. Now, he could be working on behalf of either of his parents. He might even be the one who sent the message to Lord Audley that started all of this off. However, it is equally possible that he is assisting one of his parents in covering up the crime by scaring us into stopping our search for the truth."

"Which brings us right back to start," Inga grumbled. She crossed her arms and glared at the pages. "Round and round we have been with nothing to show for our efforts. Even getting the guest list from the reception at Westminster did not help. Both Lord Ketchum and his son were there."

Dora raised her cup of coffee for a fortifying gulp, but scowled when the now cool liquid hit her tongue. "I am in need of a top-up. Shall I ring for a fresh pot?" With Inga's agreement, Dora tugged on the bellpull hanging from the wall.

Before Dora had time to sit, the hidden door swung open with a scrape. Harris leaned through the doorway and announced, "Caledonia called. She has decrypted both the message Rex received the other night, and the last of Lady Audley's old letters. She is on her way over."

Inga and Dora leapt to their feet and rushed to get changed into something more appropriate. They made it back downstairs with a minute to spare, and were ensconced in the drawing room with Rex when Caledonia rang the bell. Harris showed her in.

Caledonia entered, as always, like a breath of fresh air. She wore a linen day dress in a bright geometric print. The straight silhouette hit just below her knees, revealing her silk tights and red T-strap heels. She passed her straw cloche and leather handbag to Harris before taking up a position in front of the mantel. There, she stood at the centre of everyone's attention.

Despite her bright smile, the light powder she had dusted across her face did not completely hide the dark circles under her eyes.

"Did you stay up all night?" Dora asked, out of concern.

"I got a few hours of sleep near dawn," Caledonia said, brushing aside Dora's concern. When her explanation failed to reassure everyone, she added, "It happens sometimes. I get so caught up in solving a puzzle that I lose track of the time. I will nap this afternoon and be right as rain come tea time."

"See that you do or I will tell Grandmama to keep an eye on you," Rex warned, wagging a finger at his little sister. "Now, tell us what you discovered."

"As you know, I had one remaining letter from the stack Lord Audley found in his wife's things. The letter you sent me, Rex, was not from our blackmailer. It was written by Lady Audley."

"You owe me a pound," Inga said, elbowing her husband. "And let that be a lesson to you about the risks of betting against me."

Harris promised to pay up and waved for Caledonia to continue. It took her a moment to stop giggling before she could.

"These messages were longer than the previous ones, which worked to my benefit. With more words and letters available, I was able to fully decrypt these. I will start with the message Lady Audley sent, as I believe the other letter was the reply.

"Lady Audley had reached the limits of her patience with the matter. In her note, she says that she will not let someone else's misdeeds hang over her head for the rest of her life. The blackmailer will hardly come out smelling of roses. She is going to tell all to her husband."

"But she didn't," Rex said, interrupting his sister. "If she had, we would not be conducting this investigation. In fact, Lady Audley might still be alive."

"That is where the last letter comes in," Caledonia said. "The blackmailer was livid. He or she called Lady Audley foolish and said they did not expect much in return for keeping the secret from the world. They promised that Lady Audley and those she loved would spend the rest of their days looking over their shoulders if she didn't comply with the simple requests."

Dora's throat grew tight. The rest of Lady Audley's days proved to be much shorter than anyone could have imagined. To go from a written threat to killing someone was a major escalation, one which now seemed out of step with the letters. Dora could not help but feel they were still missing a piece of the puzzle.

"We must speak with Lord Audley again. I want to review his wife's diaries from the weeks before her death."

"We have the other investigator's notes," Inga reminded Dora. "He found nothing out of the ordinary."

"That's just it," Dora countered. "If Lady Audley didn't speak with her husband, maybe she talked to someone else. Her note specifically says that the secret is not hers. What if she visited the person the secret was about? If she were going to tell her husband everything, and risk said secret getting out, wouldn't she want to warn whoever it was about?"

"That is an excellent point." Rex rose from his chair. "We need to let Clark and Prudence know to meet us at Lord Audley's."

Chapter 20
The Other Accident

It was early enough in the day that Rex's telephone call caught Lord Audley at home. Rex took great care not to reveal anything over the line, but gave enough to convey the urgency of his request for a meeting. Lord Audley promised to clear his schedule and welcomed Rex to come round. Rex sent Archie off to deliver notes to Prudence and Clark, asking that they make their own way to Lord Audley's Mayfair home.

Dora and Rex arrived just before noon. Lord Audley awaited them in his front drawing room, wearing a crisp, white shirt, a tweed jacket, and black trousers. Rex had never seen the man without a tie around his neck, so he didn't know what to make of the scene.

Neither did Dora, apparently. She stopped in her tracks. "Your grace, where have you been hiding this casual wardrobe? Had I known, I'd have invited you along for our scavenger hunt."

"Perish the thought," Lord Audley replied. "Even in my younger years, I'd have scowled upon such ridiculous endeavours."

Clark entered the room in time to catch the end of the

conversation. He rubbed his chin as he sized up Lord Audley. "Perhaps... but something tells me you would have harnessed them to your benefit, much as we have done, your grace."

Lord Audley rocked back in his seat and barked a laugh. "Well played, Lord Clark. But you did not come here to trade barbs. Please, take a seat and let me know what you need."

"We are waiting for one more person," Clark said. "Prudence Adams is lending us her assistance."

"Ah yes, I had heard. I was not aware she was coming along today." Lord Audley asked his butler to arrange for tea and sandwiches while they waited for Prudence to join them.

The footmen arrived bearing trays just as the doorbell rang. The butler instructed them on how to arrange the side tables before leaving to open the door. He returned and ushered Prudence into the room.

Prudence entered on silent feet and bobbed her head in deference to Lord Audley. "Hello, your grace," she murmured.

"Please, come in," Audley said. "There is no need for you to stand on such ceremony. Goodness knows the rest of this lot does not. I have heard much about you and your rather unique connections within the city. I am grateful for your willingness to put them at our disposal."

Prudence's cheeks flushed at his kind words. Dora patted the seat next to hers and motioned for Prudence to take it.

Seated across from them on a settee, Rex kept a close eye on the new addition to their group. Prudence had a well-deserved reputation for staying on the outskirts of the action. Today, there was no place for her to hide. If she truly wanted to be a part of their ongoing efforts, she would have to step out of her comfort zone. Polite conversation was not going to be enough.

Would Prudence be brave enough to disagree with Lord Audley or to toss out her opinion without being asked? Rex found himself interested in seeing what she would do.

Prudence cast her gaze around the room, nodding a hello to Rex and Clark. Dora gave her no quarter to relax. She prodded Prudence with questions about her drive over, and whether she had encountered any problems along the way. The steady patter of conversation drew Prudence from her shell and got her comfortable speaking up in Lord Audley's presence. After Dora passed her a plate and offered her a cucumber sandwich, Prudence's initial reserve had all but disappeared.

Rex took a sip of his tea to wash down his sandwich and then claimed the floor. "Now that we are all here, I will share our updates so we can discuss the next steps. Our cryptographer deciphered the final two messages." Rex went on to detail the contents of each message.

Lord Audley's expression was grim by the end. "Daphne wrote that? She stood up to whoever this is? And they killed her for it?"

"Maybe," Dora said. "That remains to be seen. But let us not get ahead of ourselves. We guessed that Lady Audley did not speak with you about the situation, but can you remember whether she hinted at anything?"

Lord Audley was mystified. "If she did, I was too thick to understand what she was attempting to say."

"You and everyone else with whom she spoke," Rex reminded him. "That brings me to why we are here. May we examine your wife's diary, her correspondence, and anything else relevant from the last few months of her life?"

"You are welcome to anything in my possession. Did the previous investigator not go through them already?"

"Yes, he did, but he was searching for anomalies. We want to see which people were closest to her, and of those who she saw in her final days."

"I will ask the footmen bring them here. Do you need my help to go through them?"

Rex considered Lord Audley's offer, weighing the insights he might provide against the reticence in the man's voice. Whatever shields Audley had built over the year were proving ill equipped to deal with the newfound trauma. For Rex and the others, this was a puzzle. For Lord Audley, it meant experiencing the loss of his wife all over again.

"No, sir. We have found a good way of working together. If you don't mind, would you check back in with us later in the day? If any questions arise, we can put them aside until then."

Lord Audley sighed in relief and then coughed to cover his momentary weakness. "Very good. I will get out of your way. Will you be comfortable in here, or would you prefer to move somewhere else in the house?"

"Here is fine," Rex assured him. "We will ring for a servant should we need anything."

With that agreement in place, Lord Audley rose from his chair and rang for the butler. The man arrived so fast, Rex concluded he must have been waiting outside the room. Lord Audley conveyed the necessary instructions and then left them all to it.

The foursome partook of the sandwiches and tea, fortifying themselves for the work ahead. The butler returned with a single, mid-sized trunk, and set it on the Aubusson rug. Inside, Rex found two clothbound diaries and piles of old letters.

"How do you want to divide this up?" he asked, glancing at Dora.

"You and I can take the diaries. Prudence and Clark, that leaves you to go through the letters."

Prudence took the letters from Rex, while Clark wrinkled his nose, causing his moustache to twitch.

"Does anyone else feel like a voyeur going through all this? If someone went through my most private notes and letters, I would be mortified."

Prudence cast Clark a deadpan look. "That is because your private thoughts are mortifying. Let us all hope that Lady Audley led a more circumspect life. And at any rate, she is not here to raise any concerns."

Prudence's reminder of the loss of Lady Audley curtailed any further misbehaviour or complaint. She gathered the letters and suggested she and Clark move to the other side of the room. "We can use the gaming table to organise them as we go through."

Rex slapped his hands on his knees. "On that note, I will ring for pen and paper. Make two lists — the first of anything you think might be relevant, and the second of questions for Lord Audley."

Rex and Dora remained where they were, in the seating area nearest the fireplace. They got straight to work, hardly needing to say a word. They each knew the other's strengths and weaknesses. Dora was well adept at seeing the big picture and determining how the pieces might fit together. Therefore, she took the first pass at skimming the diaries.

Dora flagged the entries that caught her eye and then handed them over to Rex to read in further detail. Rex noted the date, any mention of other people, and a summary of the entry.

Across the room, things progressed very differently. After a while, Rex questioned whether they were progressing at all. For the first time, Clark and Prudence had to act as a team, without anyone else there to be a buffer between them. Rex laid a hand on Dora's arm and wiggled his finger toward the other pair.

Prudence had divided the letters into two piles and passed one to Clark. Perhaps had they remained divided in their tasks, all might have moved apace. Unfortunately, Prudence was determined to oversee both of their activities.

Ever since his school-boy days, Clark had chafed at having someone tell him what to do. He almost always got things done, but efficiency and order rarely played a role in it. The best way to ensure Clark's success was to get out of the way and let him do as he wanted. Though it drove his school teachers, superior officers at the war, and now leaders like Lord Audley to drink, his madcap ways endeared him to everyone else.

Everyone, that was, except Prudence Adams. Her perception of Clark was coloured by what little she had seen from the sidelines. His broad smile, gregarious ways, love of fashion, and oiled moustache made it easy to assume he was little more than a buffoon. Few saw through to the quick wit and abiding loyalty he hid underneath his jolly exterior.

When Clark shuffled through his stack and grabbed a letter at random, Prudence scowled at him. Oblivious, Clark opened the envelope with little care and tossed it aside, much more interested in the contents than the address.

Prudence gasped in horror and reached over to slap him on the hand. "Clark Kenworthy! Have a care with Lady Audley's correspondence."

Clark raised his eyes and stared at Prudence over the top of the letter. "I beg your pardon! I have done the same as you."

"You most certainly have not! Do you even know where you tossed that envelope? And take care with your hands. You are crinkling the paper!"

Clark drew himself up, retrieved the envelope and set it carefully upon the table, face down. He then set the paper aside, smoothing it of any wrinkles. That done, he waved his fingers in the air in front of Prudence's face.

"Given the warm day, I am afraid I left my gloves at home. Would you happen to have a pair in your handbag you can loan me? Preferably white silk, to match my starched white shirt."

Prudence's mouth dropped open, and she spluttered, too enraged to string together a coherent thought.

Clark took full advantage of her stupor. "No? Very well, I

will proceed barehanded, unless you want to ring for the butler and request a pair."

Prudence closed her mouth and clenched it shut to prevent herself from uttering anything else. She would be better served arguing with the portrait hanging over the mantle.

Rex bit the inside of his cheek to keep from laughing. Dora was hiding behind the open diary, pinching her nose while her shoulders shook. They struggled, but eventually won the battle for control over themselves.

After that, everyone worked quietly. It took them an hour to finish their assignments, and then another half hour to review what they had learned. Two things stood out as significant. Rex opened the drawing-room door and asked the footman positioned outside to ask Lord Audley to join them.

Lord Audley strode into the room, his gait stiff, as though he were bracing himself for the worst. He ignored the seating and chose to stand in front of the fireplace. "Did you find anything?"

"We did," Rex said. He lifted a letter covered in sprawling handwriting from the table before him. "This letter is from Lady Audley's mother, and dates to a week before your wife's death. In it, she makes mention of a scare, but promises her daughter she is recovering. She says there is no need for Lady Audley to visit. However, we can see a gap in your wife's diary shortly after. Lady Audley crossed out all her plans for the next two days, but did not write in any replacement."

"I had forgotten that. Yes, Daphne took the train to see her parents. They have an estate outside Cambridge. She visited them regularly, so I thought nothing of it."

Rex latched onto Lord Audley's choice of word. "Have? Are they still alive?"

"Lord Arrington, Daphne's father, is. Her mother passed away shortly after Daphne. Heartbroken, you see."

Rex hated to ask, but he forced the words from his mouth. "Can we ring him?"

Lord Audley wiped his hand over his mouth and rubbed his chin. "It is best if we go visit. This is too much to explain over a telephone call. I take it you all want to come along?"

"If it isn't too great an imposition," Dora said in a gentle tone. "How soon can we go?"

Lord Audley checked his watch. "Might as well go now. We can take my automobile. But first, let me telephone Lord Arrington to ensure he is at home."

A quarter of an hour later, in a tightly packed Rolls-Royce, with Lord Audley behind the wheel, the group set off from London for Cambridgeshire.

Chapter 21
A Visit to Cambridgeshire

L ord Audley navigated through the streets of London with ease, leaving Dora to wonder how often he sat behind the wheel. He seemed the type to never go anywhere without a driver. Today, however, Dora found herself uncovering her mentor's hidden depths. Either that, or this sojourn into his past was forcing him to lower his guard.

Where his walls came down, others went up. Rex had offered to sit in the front passenger seat. Dora chose the seat behind him, leaving the middle to Prudence and the other window seat to Clark. Despite the close confines of the rear bench seat, Prudence and Clark took great care to keep space between them. Yet, every jostle and bump caused their arms or legs to touch. They apologised to one another several times until the point of ridiculousness. Finally, to make them realise the futility of their efforts, Dora effected an exaggerated lean in their direction on a slight curve. Prudence ended up smashed against Clark's side. When Dora straightened, the pair glared at her in unison, sending a combined heat hot enough to burn a lesser person.

Dora, however, remained undaunted. She fluttered her

lashes at the two of them and said, "My goodness! These leather seats are so buttery soft, one cannot help but slide across them. I would apologise, but I am almost certain it will happen again."

Clark's glare faded, to be replaced by a chagrinned frown. Prudence narrowed her gaze and searched Dora's face, but soon enough, decided it was safer to back off.

That settled, Dora turned her gaze out the window. Exiting London, the scenery transformed. Verdant fields and patches of woodland lined the road, unfolding into a green expanse that stretched as far as the eye could see. Dora lowered her window a hair's breadth, allowing the fresher air, filled with the scent of grass and earth, to clear the last vestiges of soot and smoke of the city.

So, too, did it clear her mind. Dora let her focus soften until all she saw was a blur of green. Her nimble mind went to work sorting and resorting what they knew. Lady Audley was dead. Someone had blackmailed her, using the threat of revealing a secret. That secret might have been about an affair, but not one in which Lady Audley herself had taken part.

Was Lady Arrington's scary incident she referenced in her letter related? If so, how? Why did Lady Audley make her last visit? Had she gone to warn her parents to keep an eye out for trouble?

Another possibility rose to the forefront of Dora's thoughts. What if one of Lady Audley's parents was involved in the affair? Lord Arrington appeared to be the most probable candidate. The upper class turned a blind eye to straying men, mostly, but even they had their limits. If he had embarked upon an affair with someone completely unsuitable, and word got it, he would lose face. Worse yet, so, too, would Lady Audley's mother.

Dora understood a child's desire to keep their parents safe. It was why Dora had stayed far away from her family for the first four years of her life as a spy. She had not wanted to risk bringing danger to their doorstep.

In Lady Audley's shoes, Dora admitted she might have made the same choices. What was a small request here and there versus the happiness of her family? But why Lady Audley?

Dora leaned forward and pitched her voice loud enough to be heard up front. "Lord Audley, did your wife have any siblings?"

"No, she was an only child. Why do you ask?"

"Curiosity. We had not discussed the question before, and I thought there must have been a reason." Dora sidled back into her seat. For the rest of the drive, she turned the same questions over and over again. Why them? Why her?

The car slowed as they passed through a quaint village, with thatched roofs and children waving from front gardens. Lord Audley took a right turn off the main road, going onto a narrow single carriageway between hedge-lined fields. He turned again and again, letting his memory guide him in the absence of any signs.

In the distance, on a raised hill, the Arrington Estate came into view. Towering trees lined a stone drive, leading up to the impressive facade of the estate itself. Its 17th-century architecture had been designed in the English Baroque style. A large, ornate pediment capped the country home's central block. White cornerstones and window surrounds contrasted with the red brick of the building.

The stately home and the surrounding landscaped gardens conveyed an air of serenity. Pity that no one in the car shared such a mood.

Lord Audley turned the car off, but did not move. For a long moment, no one spoke while he stared at the house. Where they saw a typical country house, he saw only memories, flickering in and out like a moving picture. He took a deep breath and squared his shoulders.

The family butler, a gauntly tall man with an unexpectedly friendly smile, waited for them at the front entrance. Lord Audley led the way up one side of the double staircase leading to a stone portico with columns flanking the main door. He greeted the butler by name and received a deep bow in return.

"This way, your grace. His lordship awaits you in the book room. He remembered it always held the position as your favorite part of the house."

Dora and Rex followed Lord Audley, leaving Clark and Prudence to bring up the rear. Their heels clicked on the dark wooden floors as they walked past portraits by Lely and Kneller. The paintings must have been selected for style over anything else, as the portrait sitters bore no common features.

The book room proved to be light and airy, with white painted shelves built into the front part of the room, and a bowed window drawing light into the seating area in the back. An older man awaited them there. His hair must have once been a rich black, but now was heavily streaked with grey. He rose from his chair with the help of a cane, his dark brown eyes wide in confusion as he took in Dora, Rex, and the others.

"Lord Henry, you failed to mention you were bringing guests along," he said in a gravelled voice.

Lord Audley bowed his head. "My apologies, sir. There was too much to explain over the telephone, so I thought it best to wait until we were here."

"Now you truly have me curious. Please, all of you, have a seat. Simmons, bring in tea and cakes."

Simmons, the butler, left to do his master's bidding. One by one, Dora, Rex and the others introduced themselves to Lord Arrington before taking seats. They filled every place in the small sitting area. Dora and Rex sat together on one of the matching settees, as they usually did. Clark and Prudence landed again in close quarters on the other. Lord Arrington kept his place in a wingback chair, leaving Lord Audley to lay claim to an elaborately carved accent chair upholstered in watered blue silk.

After the butler arrived with tea, Dora took charge of pouring and distributing cups. When all was settled, Lord Arrington addressed the room.

"I get so few visitors nowadays that I am want to complain. Between the short notice and worry lines marring your face, Lord Henry, I take it this is not a social visit. Please, tell me why you are here."

Lord Audley nodded his head and began the explanation. He spoke in starts and stops, halting when the topic became too difficult. When Dora could take it no more, she leapt in during an overlong pause.

"We found a letter from your wife, sent to your daughter, shortly before her death. She mentioned a scare. Do you recall what happened?"

Lord Arrington's brow creased in concentration. "Ah yes, it was a small thing. Certainly not worth Daphne making the trip to see us. Charlotte, Lady Arrington, that is, twisted her ankle while walking in the gardens. She tripped over a loose stone and stumbled. A few days of rest set the bruises and joint to rights."

Dora's spirits sank. That hardly sounded suspicious. Still, instinct told her they had to be on the right track. "How did your daughter seem during her last visit?"

"Preoccupied. She spent most of the time with her mother, although that was far from unusual. The two always had a strong bond."

"Do you have any idea what they discussed? Did your wife say anything to you afterward?"

"No. Charlotte was quiet, thoughtful. Looking back, it was

almost as though she were steeling herself for something. Then we got word of Daphne's accident. Charlotte fell apart. I did not see any point in prying. Whatever it was, it became irrelevant. Charlotte wandered around like a ghost in the hallways and gardens. Each day, her heart broke a little more until she collapsed in the bower. By the time we found her, it was too late."

The anguish in the man's voice brought tears to Dora's eyes. A quick glance confirmed the others were just as moved. A dozen questions leapt to her mind. Had Lady Arrington suffered from devastation or guilt? Was Lord Arrington the one to blame for both women dying? More and more questions, each less appropriate than the other. Had the man been anyone other than Lord Audley's father-in-law, Dora would not have hesitated to ask pointed questions.

She backtracked and took a different route. "If it is not too painful, can you tell us more about Lady Daphne? If nothing else, it will help us get a fuller picture of who she was."

Lord Arrington's expression softened, though his eyes still held the sheen of wetness. "Daphne exhibited beauty, kindness, and became the greatest blessing of our lives. I was not blind to her faults, for she was human and fallible, but the good far outweighed the bad.

"When my wife told me she was increasing, I — well, I could hardly believe it. After so many years. She was almost afraid to tell me, but she need not have feared. I could never deprive her of anything, least of all a child. Our child," he added.

Prudence reached over and offered Lord Arrington a hand. "I have keenly felt the pain of great loss, my lord. That is why I offered to help the others. I promise, if someone was behind your daughter's death, we will find them and ensure they pay for their crime."

The old man squeezed Prudence's hand as he choked back a sob. The men all glanced away, to give him the space to get his emotions under control.

Dora bided her time before making a request. "Do you have any portraits of your wife and daughter?"

"Yes, we had a family portrait made when Daphne debuted. It is hanging in the front drawing room. Would you like to see it?"

"If it won't pain you overmuch. We can go on our own, if that is easier."

"The movement will do me good, or so the doctors tell me. And resting my eyes upon the faces of my dearest loves is never a hardship. Those memories that come to mind are all I have left of them."

Prudence slid her arm through Lord Arrington's after he rose from his chair. She let him think he was escorting her, when in reality she helped steady his gait. The others hung back, allowing him to take the lead at his own pace. He guided them out of the reading room and back toward the front entrance. Another door stood off to the side. It opened into a spacious drawing room with yellow papered walls and floral fabrics covering the chairs.

It was the grand portrait hanging over the fireplace mantle that captured Dora's full attention. At the centre, Lord Arrington stood with an air of dignified authority, his posture upright, exuding a sense of pride and responsibility. His hair was still ebony, but already grey crept in at his temples. To his right, Lady Arrington sat gracefully on an ornate upholstered chair. Her expression was serene, with a gentle smile playing on her lips. With her pale blonde hair, she could have been a relative to Rex and Caledonia. Given the close ties amongst the English upper class, perhaps she was.

Lady Daphne stood slightly in front of her parents, her

youth and vivacity bringing a spark of energy to the composition. Her chestnut hair was styled in an elaborate up-do, adorned with flowers that caught the light, adding a touch of brightness to the scene. Her eyes were bright, looking out at the viewer with anticipation and a hint of the independence she was beginning to assert.

Dora studied the painting, moving closer to get a better view. She counted the similarities between mother and daughter, their connection as obvious as between Dora and her family. But when it came to Lord Arrington, there the task become much more difficult. There was no hint of his broad nose or cleft chin, nor his dark good looks. He was the odd man out.

Dora's heart raced as she realised what Lady Audley's secret had been.

Chapter 22
The Eavesdropper

To say that Rex's confidence had grown by leaps and bounds since Dora took him under her wing would be a vast understatement. Although he was not quite up to the level of Inga, he was certain he could follow her trains of thought. Yet, when she spun around in the drawing room and speared Lord Arrington with a heated glare, Rex did not know why.

"Did you know?" she asked.

"Yes. I had always known," Lord Arrington replied.

Dora shifted her gaze to Lord Audley. "And you? Did you keep this from us?"

"Keep what?" Clark muttered. Prudence elbowed him to keep quiet.

"I have no idea what you are talking about," Lord Audley replied, showing more patience than Rex felt.

"Lord Arrington is not Daphne's father."

"I was not her natural father, you mean. But in every other way, she was mine," Lord Arrington stated, leaving no room for discussion.

"How did you guess that?" Clark asked, voicing the words in Rex's head.

Dora gestured to the portrait hanging on the wall. "I am certain you must have studied science in school, Lord Clark. Children are usually a mix of both of their parents. But if you look closely, you will see that Lady Daphne has no features in common with Lord Arrington. Therefore, I could only assume that she was illegitimate. That was the affair that we heard about, wasn't it? Not one had by Lord or Lady Audley, but by your wife a generation earlier."

Lord Arrington bristled, but one glance at his son-in-law's stern gaze had him backing down. His shoulders slumped in defeat. "I can see that you're not going to leave here without a full explanation, and given the reason you are asking, I suppose one is deserved. I'm afraid my old bones need to rest. Sit down and I will start from the beginning."

The group sat in the nearest cluster of seating, with Lord Arrington choosing the chair with the best view of the portrait. Prudence and Lord Audley flanked him, while Rex and Dora sat across from the man so they could monitor his body language and facial expressions. Clark alone remained standing, choosing to lean against the side of Dora's wingback chair.

Despite his offer to tell everything, Lord Arrington remained stubbornly silent. Rex had the sense he was searching his memories for where to start. Lord Audley finally intervened.

"From what I could see, you and Lady Arrington had a happy marriage. I must admit I am surprised to learn she stepped out."

"We did, although our happiness came with time," Lord Arrington replied. "Like you and Daphne, our decision to marry was based on logic rather than emotion. We had similar views on how and where to spend our time, rubbed along well enough, and saw the benefit of tying our two families together. Chief amongst our desires was that to have children. We dreamed of a busy nursery, and watching sons and daughters play chase in the garden."

"But you struggled to conceive," Dora said.

Lord Arrington nodded. "After several years passed, we were forced to face the reality that one of us was at fault. I know the easy solution is to blame the woman, but I suspected I was the problem, because of a childhood accident. That is the only reason my wife strayed. It was with my blessing, and with my promise that I would acknowledge any resulting child as my own."

While Lord Arrington spoke with a no-nonsense tone, Rex struggled to accept the explanation. Inheritance lines were sacrosanct. Wives were expected to provide an heir and a spare, and only then might the husband and society at large turn a blind eye to her dalliances.

"What if the child had been a son?" Rex asked, giving voice to his thoughts.

"It made no difference to me, at first. But I will admit to feeling a great relief when my wife gave birth to a daughter. When I held Daphne, it was love at first sight. She was mine, and no one could tell me otherwise. Our shared love for our daughter strengthened our marriage into what you saw, Lord Henry."

Lord Audley nodded. "I cannot remember you and Lady Arrington ever having a cross word with one another."

"We were not perfect," Lord Arrington replied. "But we were wise enough to settle any disagreements away from prying eyes and listening ears."

"Agreements and disagreements, both," Lord Audley said. "I never caught wind of any questions about Daphne's parentage. Tell me, how did you keep this a secret? Who was her father?"

"I do not know for certain. My wife did not want to risk any rancour, so she kept mum about it."

"Come now, you must have held some inkling," Clark said, challenging the man's statement.

Lord Arrington glanced at the portrait and then lowered his head, as though asking forgiveness for what he was about to say. "It was a delicate situation, as you can imagine. It had to be someone equal in status, and trustworthy. There was only one man who I thought possible of the role. He was a childhood friend of my wife, a very dear friend who had already wed and had an heir."

"The old Lord Ketchum," Dora blurted.

"What?" Clark shifted around the chair to stare Dora in the face. "What makes you say that?"

Once again, Rex's thoughts were in line with Dora's. He answered, "Theodora is right, isn't she? Our search keeps coming back to the Ketchum family. The current Lady Ketchum is American, and did not come to England until it was time for her to marry. Her father would have had no chance to cross paths with Lord Arrington's wife a generation earlier. But old Lord Ketchum — the elder lord, father of the current Lord Ketchum — fits the age and profile."

"Yes," Lord Arrington agreed. "Although I cannot imagine how his son came to find out, nor why he would use this information against Daphne. She posed no threat to him."

"I found out because my father told me," a man said in a deep baritone.

Rex twisted in his chair and saw that a middle-aged man stood in the drawing-room doorway. His chestnut hair was unquestionably the same shade as Lady Audley's had been. Rex felt certain he was the same man who had knocked into him at Westminster. But how had he found them? And what was he doing here?

"Lord Ketchum!" Lord Arrington gasped, giving the new arrival a name. The old man paled and clutched at his chest. "What are you doing here and how did you get in?"

"I have been following the trail of this group for days, ever since I overhead you asking questions about Lady Audley at Westminster. You cannot take a hint, can you? As to how I got in, your footman opened the door. I stopped him before he could announce my arrival. Don't worry, I am sure he will recover from the light knock on his head."

Rex froze in place. Lord Ketchum's lackadaisical tone stood in sharp contrast to the picture his words created. Rex lifted one hand and motioned for everyone to remain still.

Lord Ketchum swaggered into the room, his hands in his jacket pockets. "Since you ignored all my warnings to back off this matter and to let it be, we find ourselves here. Perhaps if you know the truth, you will finally stop looking into ancient history.

"On his deathbed, my father made me promise I would keep watch over my younger sister — a sister I never knew I had. It was the first time I ever saw him express concern for anyone. He certainly never bothered to watch over me. When I dared to ask for help, he told me that being a man meant taking control over situations. Even when I suffered the pain of relentless bullying during my school years, my pleas for help went ignored. He never lifted a finger for me, but with his dying breath, he begged me to care for her."

"And so you did the opposite?" Lord Audley asked. His voice was low, but Rex did not miss the sharp edge. "You blackmailed my wife!"

"You make it sound so terrible," Lord Ketchum replied. "She was my sister. My own flesh and blood. I learned all about her — her pastimes, pleasures, and habits. I'd had to marry a bloody American to save my family from ruin. A no one with no lineage! And her, my sister, had everything. Money, privilege, and the future honour of becoming a duchess. If anything, she should have helped me. Yet, when I approached her, she pled ignorance. She told me to take my lies away. Just like my father — she refused to listen, to do what was right. I had no choice but to force her hand."

"What did you want from her?" Audley growled. "Money? Power?"

Lord Ketchum pulled his left hand free from his pocket and waved off Lord Audley's comments. "I asked so little of her. My wife needed introductions to society. Your were on the rise. I asked her to ensure you brought me along. I offered her simple ways to keep her secret. She was the one who acted foolishly."

Rex forced his gaze away from Lord Ketchum to check how the other were reacting. Prudence was so aghast that her mouth hung open. Clark and Dora both bore flushed faces as they struggled to contain their ire. Lord Arrington had paled. Only Lord Audley appeared unmoved.

That appearance was deceiving. Rex had come to know the man well enough to recognise that the tick in his jaw muscle and the narrowed gaze indicated his temper was close to boiling.

Prudence finally closed her mouth, only to open it again to launch a volley of her own. "How can you be so blasé? You killed a woman. Have you no regrets?"

Lord Ketchum drew himself up. "I did not raise my hand against anyone. They ran from me."

"'They?" Prudence spluttered.

Dora leaned forward. "Lady Arrington's accident in the garden. You were there. Did she refuse to kowtow to your wishes? Did she tumble over, or did you shove her down?"

Lord Ketchum held up a hand to stop Dora. "How dare you! Do not lay the blame for any of this on my doorstep. Do you think I wanted them dead? Tell me how have I profited in their absence?"

Lord Ketchum's question hung in the air. Rex found he had no answer. The man made an excellent point. Rex and the others had looked into Lord Ketchum's background. He had never advanced past the middle of the pack. He had only what his title and place in society gave him.

But that did not excuse his actions. His intention had been to manipulate Lady Audley and her mother into boosting his reputation.

Rex did not have to search far to find Ketchum's opposite. Dora had shed her heritage and built a new identity from scratch. Lord Audley worked long into the night to ensure England's safety and status as a world power. Yet, much of what he did took place in the shadows.

"Tell me what happened to my wife," Lord Audley growled. "Prove your innocence, if you can."

"Her riding schedule was hardly a secret. I contrived to cross her path. I spoke in a reasonable tone, but she hurled accusations my way, just as you are doing now. She told me to stay away from her mother."

"You did not stop there, though, did you?"

"She took off, and I gave chase. I shouted for her to slow down, but the wind carried my words away. If she heard them, she gave no sign. I urged my horse to lengthen its stride. When I got within reach, I lashed out with my crop, intending to startle her horse into slowing its pace." Lord Ketchum's voice trailed off and he stared into the distance. "Everyone knew she excelled at horsemanship. And yet, when the horse bucked, she tumbled off its back, like a child on their first day in the saddle. What could I do?"

"Seek help," Prudence answered. "Maybe if you have stopped to check on her, or called for aid, Lady Audley would still be alive. Make no mistake, Lord Ketchum. From where I sit, you are fully responsible for her death."

"And that of her mother," Lord Arrington added. "Losing Daphne devastated us both, but now I understand my wife carried an additional burden. If she had only let me in, had shared that burden with me...." He stopped there, too choked to finish his thought.

"Even you recognise that your family bears culpability," Lord Ketchum murmured. He walked closer to the group and directed his next words at Lord Audley. "Let us be done with all this. No more games, no more discussions. The past is what it is, for all of us."

Rex's heart sank. Every fibre of his being called for justice, but what could they do? They possessed such a minimal amount of evidence for a case that had long become cold. They achieved a miracle by solving it. Getting justice remained beyond reach.

Lord Audley refused to give up. "Lord Ketchum, you forget yourself. We are no longer young men, scrabbling for power and money. While your star failed to rise, mine sits at the pinnacle of the sky. I will use every ounce of my sway, every coin in my bank, to gather the proof that you were there the day Daphne died." He rose from his seat and widened his stance, showing he would not go quietly into the night.

"Then you leave me no choice," Lord Ketchum replied. He pulled his right hand from his coat pocket. In it, he held a small, black pistol. But he did not aim it at Lord Audley. Instead, he stretched out his arm and aimed squarely at Lord Arrington.

The old man trembled, but he did not duck or hide.

"If Lord Arrington is gone, there will be no one left to testify to Daphne's illegitimacy. You can show our paths crossed all you want, but without proof of any connection between us, who will believe you?"

Rex sized up the situation in an instant. From where he sat, stopping Lord Ketchum was impossible. He stood too far away.

The same for Lord Audley. The man's tightly clenched fists testified to how hard he was working to hold himself back.

Lord Ketchum's face shifted, any sign of fear or concern taking a back seat to his determination. He gritted his teeth and tightened his grip on the gun.

At that moment, Clark launched into motion. He was the closest to Lord Ketchum, the only one standing, and their only hope of saving Lord Arrington from death. Without a moment of hesitation, Clark sprang forward and shoved Lord Ketchum off balance.

As Lord Ketchum fell, he pulled the trigger. The bang far outsized the small handgun. Rex's ears rang, or perhaps that was Prudence's scream. The whole world ceased to move for an instant.

Then Lord Ketchum hit the floor, with Clark sprawled atop him. Clark pulled back his fist and crashed it into Ketchum's face, breaking his nose with an audible crunch. His head bounced against the floor and he stopped moving.

Prudence cried out again. Rex swung his head around to find her fluttering her hands over Lord Arrington. The right sleeve of the man's coat grew darker with every minute.

Dora leapt to her feet and rushed over. Without a word, she pulled the scarf from around her neck and wrapped it around Lord Arrington's arm. She worked with the quiet expertise of a battle-hardened nurse.

From there, the world snapped back into motion. In seconds, servants overran the drawing room. Someone called for the doctor, another brought water and towels. Lord Audley took responsibility for keeping Lord Ketchum under guard.

Hours later, they returned to London. No one spoke on the drive home. All of them were too occupied pondering what could have happened if Clark had not acted quickly. When they reached Mayfair, Lord Audley offered his thanks. To a one, they waved them off.

There had been too much death, too great of suffering, and too high a price paid for one man's desperate attempts to achieve greatness.

Chapter 23
All Becomes Clear

A week passed by with no word from Lord Audley. Dora and Rex invited Clark and Prudence to dinner, and took great amusement at watching the pair spar over every topic of conversation. Now that their sleuthing days were over, any sense of camaraderie was gone.

Dora was certain something lay underneath Clark and Prudence's fiery disputes, and with little else to entertain her, she enjoyed winding them up and seeing where they went.

Outside, the summer days grew ever shorter. Soon, the leaves would flame red, fade to orange, and then tumble to the ground. Parliament would return to session. Dora and Rex would find a new assignment. But one last question remained about the mystery of Lady Audley's death. Who had sent Lord Audley the anonymous note that brought the past into the present?

When Lord Audley invited Dora and Rex to come round one afternoon, Dora suspected they would soon find out. Yet, when his staid old butler led them to the drawing room, Lord Audley sat alone.

Dora availed herself of the chair directly across from her mentor. She examined the man's face for any indication of his emotional state. He still had shadows under his eyes, and his complexion was in need of the outdoors, but his shoulders no longer sagged. He was grieving, but the hint of lightness in his being gave her hope.

"We are expecting a guest in half an hour's time, so if you don't mind, we will proceed with business and enjoy tea later. Is that acceptable?" Lord Audley asked.

Dora and Rex gave a nod of approval.

"I will begin by expressing my thanks again for your efforts to unmask Daphne's killer. Despite Lord Ketchum's claims of an accident, I will forever hold him responsible."

"You are right to do so," Dora said. "His behaviour was reprehensible, and all the subsequent losses lie at his doorstep. If there was any doubt that he had lost the plot entirely, his plan to murder Lord Arrington in front of all of us proves it. How is Lord Arrington, by the way?"

"The old man is made of sterner stuff than most. He is recuperating at home, under the watchful eyes of his butler and housekeeper. Lord Ketchum will spend the rest of his days behind bars. I made sure of it, by providing the sentencing judge with a full picture of his criminal activity."

Dora found that to be a fitting end for someone who had cut short so many other lives.

Lord Audley took a deep, cleansing breath and exhaled it in a whoosh. "Enough of the distasteful matters. I am in your debt. Tell me, what boon can I offer?"

"You are not in our debt, sir," Dora replied. "We gave our help freely, with no expectation of a reward. There can be no tally of debts paid and owed amongst friends and family. After all these years, after all we have been through as a team, we are related by all but blood. As we have seen with Lord and Lady Arrington, there are many ties that bind families together."

Lord Audley had always been a master at disguising his sentiment behind a cool mask of indifference. But in the wake of Dora's heartfelt words, he allowed the mask to drop and for Dora and Rex to see the man behind it. His eyes took on a sheen of tears, and his salt and pepper moustache quivered as he fought for control. Without a moment of thought to question her decision, Dora leapt to her feet and threw her arms around her mentor. Despite the awkward lean of hugging a man sitting down, she held on tight. He breathed a ragged sigh and squeezed her once before sliding his arms free. By the time she stood, his face was again impassive.

"Enough of that. We have little time and more important matters to discuss. What are your opinions of Lord Clark and Miss Adams after working closely with them?"

Dora took her seat and glanced at Rex. They had discussed the matter several times and were in full agreement. However, it was not their opinions that counted right now.

As previously agreed, Rex was the one who replied. "Our position remains unchanged. Both Clark and Prudence acquitted themselves well. Though they will need training, the same held true for the two of us. But that matters not at all unless you agree with our suggestion to bring them on board. Where do you stand on this matter?"

Lord Audley smoothed his moustache into place while pondering the matter. Dora did not believe for an instant that he was undecided. The man always thought three moves ahead. Yet, he held his silence until Dora could hardly stand it a moment longer.

He cleared his throat. "I had one rule when I founded this line of secret agents working on behalf of the crown — men only. Unaccompanied men who could move in and out of places, with no entanglements to trip them up or pull them down. Then you, Dora, strode into my home and demanded a chance to prove yourself. I could not say no to your suggestion of bringing Inga as your companion. Your household has grown by leaps and bounds over the years. What I always viewed as a weakness is your greatest strength. You and Rex, Inga and Harris, Cynthia and the twins... despite being a veritable travelling army, your stealth is undeniable."

"Thank you," Dora said, acknowledging the compliment with a bow of her head. "But what does that have to do with Clark and Prudence?"

"I am getting to that," Lord Audley replied, rolling his eyes at her impudence. "I agreed to consider Clark for the role of my heir-apparent. Prudence took a cue from your book and barged her way through the door. Five years ago, I would have tossed Prudence out on her ear. But not now, not after seeing all you have accomplished. So, I have a proposal. Although it pertains to Prudence and Clark, it falls to the two of you to decide. I would bring them on as a package deal. I will take Clark under my wing and teach him everything I know. You, Dora, will do the same for Prudence. But they must sign on to being a team for as long as Prudence remains in service. They do not have to go so far as you and Rex have done, but a cordial working relationship is the bare minimum. Knowing this, will they accept?"

Dora fought back the urge to say yes. Although she felt certain Prudence would say yes, she was less confident regarding Clark. She turned to Rex, seeking his opinion on the matter. For his part, Rex had adopted a contemplative stance. His gaze had softened, and he rubbed his fingers together, fiddling wordlessly while he considered the question.

The longer he remained silent, the more determined Dora

became to hear him say yes. Clark needed a calling. Like them, he needed to matter for something he did, and not because of his eventual title. More than that, he needed a safe outlet for his creative mind, or else he would spend the rest of his days causing chaos for the sheer entertainment value.

Rex reached the same conclusion. "Clark is no fool, despite how the world sees him. If we explain it to him, just as you have done for us now, he will see reason."

"I expect you are right," Lord Audley agreed. "I will leave it to the two of you to approach Prudence and Clark in the best way you see fit. You have my permission to tell them whatever you feel comfortable sharing about yourselves and how you came to be involved."

The ornate grandfather clock hanging on the wall chimed the half hour. Lord Audley got up and rang for the servants. His butler appeared within moments.

"Yes, your grace?"

"Our visitor should arrive momentarily. Please see her in when she does. And can you please have a one of the footmen bring tea?"

"Of course, your grace." The butler bowed and then departed to do his master's bidding.

The tea service arrived before the guest, but not by much. Dora hardly had time to offer to play mother before the butler cleared his throat in the doorway and announced the new arrival.

"Lady Ketchum is here, your grace."

Lady Ketchum walked into the room on silent feet. She was still a wisp of a woman, but she stood taller than when Dora had met her at her mother's home. Like Lord Audley, her face bore shadows and her lips were thin, but her light brown hair hung loose down her back.

"Good afternoon, Lord Audley, Lord Rex, and Miss Laurent. Thank you for seeing me."

Lord Audley motioned for her to take a seat. Dora poured tea and passed cups around. A strange energy filled the room, but it wasn't anger. Lady Ketchum was not here to remonstrate them for seeing her husband sent to prison.

Lord Audley took a sip of his tea and then rested his china cup on a nearby side table. He turned to Lady Ketchum. "If you're okay with it, let's skip the pleasantries and talk about the obvious issue. I had intended to get in contact, but your message beat mine, Lady Ketchum. Unless I am mistaken, you are the one who clued me in about your husband's duplicitous behaviour."

Lady Ketchum took a deep breath before answering. "I am sure you think me perfectly awful for not coming forward with the truth."

"Nothing of the sort," Lord Audley assured her. "Rex, Theodora, and I recognise the fraught nature of your position. That you did anything at all to alert me to this matter is more than I would expect. For certain, you would have only benefitted by holding your tongue."

"That is not quite true," Lady Ketchum replied. She bit her lip, weighing whether to say more.

Somehow, Dora did not believe Lady Ketchum had kept this secret for so many years. "When did you discover your husband's connection to Lady Audley?"

"This summer. My son, Felix, came down from Oxford. I overheard my husband speaking with him. He was training him on how to progress through to the highest echelons of society. He told him to use every tool available and cited his relationship to Lady Audley. My husband said her death had been an accident, and with the loss of her, so too disappeared his best chance of increasing his power. He coached Felix to tread more carefully, and to not make the same mistake."

Dora clenched her hands into a fist to prevent a shudder from rocking her body. How could the man have been so callous as to speak of Lady Audley's death with such innocence, knowing he was to blame?

"I had to act, you see," Lady Ketchum continued. "Felix is young yet, and can still choose a different path in life. But with his father guiding him, he would only end up as a rotten egg. I did not wish that on my child."

"How did you know for certain your husband was involved in Lady Audley's death?" Dora asked.

"I did not, at first. But there was an edge to his tone that day that sat wrong. The thought refused to release its grasp on me. When he and Felix went away for a weekend, I claimed to be ill and remained behind. I searched through his study, in all the hiding places he thought I did not know existed. I found the letter — the one I later sent to you, Lord Rex. I still had an old one from Lady Audley. The handwriting was a match. That was when I decided to borrow from their bag of tricks and send a note of my own."

"And well you did, my lady," Lord Audley said, nodding his head in acknowledgement of her bravery. "Please, tell me if there is anything I can do to assist you and your son during this difficult time."

"Guide him as best as you can, but perhaps from a distance for a while. He does not fully understand what happened and is weighed down by youthful resentment. He blames you for tarnishing the family name, blithely ignoring his father's leading role in the matter. I will work on him, a little every day, until I can chip away the hard shell my husband fostered and reveal the young man I know lives inside."

Lord Audley promised to act as an invisible hand, and open

doors where he could. If there was one lesson to take away from this, it was that the sins of the father should not burden their young.

Only time would tell whether Lord Felix Ketchum would carve a new path for his family legacy.

Epilogue

The driver pulled the Rolls-Royce to a stop in front of the illustrious Mayfair home of the Dowager Duchess of Rockingham. Lord Audley hesitated before exiting the car. Though he had faced many a tough audience in his years as a peer in the House of Lords, a foreign policy expert, and a leader on the front lines, this particular afternoon found him suffering from nerves.

Inside the home, Lady Edith and Lady Caledonia awaited his arrival. They could hardly be classed as the enemy, but that did not mean Lord Audley was on safe ground. One wrong word — indeed, one misstep — could see his brilliant plan explode into nothing.

Treating the pair of intelligent women like enemy combatants on a field of battle would be the worst mistake he could make. So he took a page from Dora's book, inhaling and exhaling five long breaths, until his heart beat at a steady, sedate pace.

The driver exited the car and opened Lord Audley's door. He stood tall in his dark suit and cap, his appearance proclaiming his passenger as someone important. The duke rose from his seat, asked the driver to wait, and then strode up to the dowager's front door with his head held high.

He rang the bell once and waited hardly anytime at all before Sheffield invited him inside.

"May I take your coat and hat, your grace?" The butler motioned for a footman to step forward to ferry the items to a nearby cupboard.

Lord Audley handed them over, allowing the rote mannerisms of a society visit to further steady his nerves. The butler showed him the drawing room and announced his arrival before taking his departure.

The women sat beside one another on an antique settee. A low table placed in front of them stood ready to hold the tea tray. Clearly, the single armchair across from them was meant for him. At the butler's announcement, the women rose from their seats to welcome him. They were of a similar height, and the family resemblance was there in the shape of their faces. But where Lady Edith's hair had gone white with age, Caledonia remained a radiant blonde.

"Good afternoon, ladies," he said, giving a slight bow in their direction. Lady Edith inclined her head in acknowledgement, while Caledonia bobbed a curtsy. Though not entirely inappropriate given his title, it was certainly unexpected. One glance at the cheeky smile on her face gave all the explanation he needed. The irrepressible Dora was rubbing off on her new sister-in-law.

"Please have a seat, Lord Audley. May I pour you a cup of tea?" Lady Edith asked. He acquiesced and she played mother. The antique clock on the mantle ticked off the minutes. The social niceties that had grounded him earlier now dragged on, grating on his nerves.

His visit was Important, with a capital I. He wasn't some young swain come calling on the season's debutante. It was time he remembered that. So, with only minor trepidation, he skipped right past the staid conversations about the weather and on to the purpose of his visit.

"Do either of you mind if I get to the heart of the matter?" he asked.

"I wish you would," Caledonia replied, shifting excitedly in her seat. "Rex said you wanted to speak with me before I make my application to university. I've been on pins and needles ever since, wondering what you will say."

"As have I," Edith added, although her steely gaze promised retribution should Lord Audley step out of line.

"I come in peace, I promise," he said to assuage the older woman's nerves. "Please, get comfortable, as to understand my suggestion, I will first need to tell you a story."

Caledonia's eyes sparkled in delight as she settled in beside her grandmother on the settee.

"To ensure the safety of our great nation, our government employs a department of code breakers. While our enemies suspect such a department exists, the names of the individuals employed there stay hidden. During the war, their efforts proved invaluable in helping our troops prepare for battles and avoid sneak attacks. Although these individuals rarely left our shores, they saved thousands of lives.

"After the war ended, most of these individuals returned to their ordinary lives. A rare few, however, remained. Much like Dora and Rex, they lead a double life. To the wider world, they are teachers, office workers, and even men and women of leisure. Within the four walls of their department, they put their prodigious minds to work decoding messages of a different type."

Lady Edith raised a hand. "I do not understand, Lord Audley. Are you suggesting that someone is planning for another war, even as we speak?"

"It would be more accurate to say that we hope to avoid that outcome."

"They are working on diplomatic messages," Caledonia said with a gasp. "That's it, isn't it? It is the same reason you send people like my brother and Dora into the field. Decisions are taken in government halls, alliances struck behind closed doors, long before anyone lifts a weapon."

"Exactly." Lord Audley was impressed by how quickly Caledonia leapt to the right conclusion. "That is why I am here today. Our country has a great need of bright minds to work here. I have spoken with a few of them, and noted the commonalities in their skills and training. Love of puzzles is a must, as you have already seen the time and dedication required to decipher hidden messages. Beyond that, the department looks for linguists, musicians, and mathematicians."

"People like me?" Caledonia shifted forward, giving Lord Audley her full attention. "Women?"

"Yes, even women. Despite what many would have us think, brilliance is not limited to the males of our species. I can thank Dora for pointing this out to me five years ago."

Lord Audley shifted his attention to the dowager. She had laced her fingers together, and rested them on her lap. Audley recognised this as her position for negotiation. Caledonia's enthusiasm for the prospect was clear, but without her grandmother's blessing, the conversation would end there.

"I will not see my granddaughter chained to a desk, Audley, with her gifts hidden from the world. She deserves better than that."

"I agree. In fact, I insist she remain in plain sight, just like Rex and Dora."

"*Just like them?*" Edith asked.

"I am not suggesting Caledonia undertake risky missions," he clarified. "Caledonia wants to go to university. I say it is an excellent decision. I have every confidence she will soar in the rigorous academic environment. If she is showered with prizes and glory, all the better." He shifted his gaze to the young woman. "I assume you intend to continue your musical studies?"

Caledonia nodded. "Yes, along with European languages."

"Consider adding maths to your course list. You need not go so far as a dual degree, but a firm grounding in their logical approach to problem solving and pattern identification will be of great use."

"And after she matriculates?" Lady Edith asked.

"She can take on whatever career or indulge in whatever interests she would like. Part of her days, however, I would like her to spend on an internship with the code breaking team. I have a specific mentor in mind, one with whom Caledonia is certain to find many shared interests."

Caledonia cut in. "Who is he?"

"Her name," Audley replied, "is a secret until the day you are introduced in person."

Caledonia crossed her arms and rocked back, her frustration clear.

Lady Edith shook her head at her granddaughter. "Let us move on to discussions of safety. My family has already put one member at risk. I dislike the idea of giving the government a second tribute."

"Tell me, Lady Edith, can you name any of our code breakers? Your knowledge of secrets is prodigious. Surely you can come up with one name."

Lady Edith wrinkled her brow, thinking for a long moment, before shaking her head. "I see your point. But how can you ensure this will remain the case? Now, we can all remember the horrors of war. But what about as time goes on? The younger generations are unscathed, thank goodness, but this too has a cost. Will they grasp the necessity of keeping quiet?"

"Secrecy is ensured in two ways. The first, by the individuals themselves. They tell no one what they do, because it could cost them their lives. They are not fools. The second way we uphold silence is through laws. Should anyone breathe a word of what they do, they will find the full force of His Majesty's force raised against them."

"I want to sign up now," Caledonia interjected. "Why can I not begin training while I do my studies?"

"Your training will be your studies. Go to Oxford as you intend. You will ace the entrance exams. I will provide you with a letter of support to ensure you land in the right place. There, the best thing you can do is to throw your whole self into your education. When you have completed your degree, I will ask you again if you want to go into service. If your answer is still yes, we will discuss next steps."

Caledonia glanced at her grandmother. "What say you, Grandmama? Lord Audley has answered all your questions, and hopefully laid your concerns to rest. He has demanded nothing of me which I would not do anyway."

"That last part is the most important," Lady Edith answered. She turned to Lord Audley. "The greatest blessing and biggest challenge one faces when viewing children and grandchildren is the realisation that they have inherited your best and worst traits. Rex and Caledonia both are far too pig-headed to allow me to stand in their way. Given I was the same at their age, I can hardly complain. But they are both smart, dedicated, and honest. These are traits I believe we all share. That will have to be my consolation."

Caledonia huffed at her grandmother's words. "Is that a yes, Grandmama? Does it pain you so much to come right out and say it?"

Lady Edith unlaced her fingers and reached out an arm to wrap around her granddaughter's shoulders. She pulled the young woman tight against her, paying no mind to the wrinkles she was putting into her dress. "For you, my dearest girl, my answer is always a yes. But I hope you will not hold against me my desire to keep you safe."

"Our greatest treasures must always be protected," Lord Audley agreed. "Like you, I count Caledonia as one of them. There is strength in numbers. I will use my influence to keep her safe, and Rex and Dora will lend their support as well. In this, you have my enduring promise."

"Then it is decided... at least for now," Caledonia announced. She leaned her head against her grandmother's shoulder. "Really, Grandmama, you do not carry all the blame for our wayward paths. From what I have seen in my research into our family history, the passion for puzzles harkens back several generations."

"What research is this?" Lord Audley asked. "Are you referring to that trove of diaries you discovered in the attic?"

"Indeed, I am. Best I can tell, it all started with Lady Grace and Lord Roland. It was 1813. Our soldiers battled across the continent in their efforts to defeat Napoleon. Here in England, the Duke of Northumberland suffered the death of his heir, causing the responsibility to skip down a generation. That is where Roland comes in — Lord Roland Percy, Earl Percy, heir to the Northumberland dukedom."

Caledonia stopped there, but Lord Audley urged her to tell more. He was in no rush, and if anything, he was keen to learn more, given Caledonia's earlier remark. Lady Edith added her encouragement.

"Lord Percy came to London with the plan to marry, a condition dictated by his grandfather. He set his sights on the Incomparable — the so-called Diamond of the First Water."

"I am so glad that title went out of fashion," Edith said with a sigh. "True beauty goes far deeper than the surface. Based on your tone, I take it things didn't go to plan for young Roland, or else this will be a remarkably short story."

Caledonia laughed. "They most certainly did not. You see, the Diamond, as she was called, went missing. Queen Charlotte issued an edict to Lord Roland, that he had to find her missing favourite. Lady Grace, the best friend of the missing girl, stepped in to help."

"Well?" Lord Audley asked, leaning forward. "Did they find her?"

Caledonia shrugged. "I don't know yet. I am only about a third of the way through the tale, as it is written in starts and stops in Lady Grace's diaries. Her handwriting leaves much to be desired, so it is slow going."

Lady Edith huffed and Lord Audley growled, both so caught up in the story that they hated to be left hanging. Before their visit drew to a close, they made Caledonia promise to fill them in once she uncovered the full details of what happened to the missing diamond.

As for Caledonia's future, that remains unwritten...
for now...

* * *

Discover the Crown Jewels Mystery series - where intrepid duos solve crimes at the highest levels of Regency society.

Book 1: THE MISSING DIAMOND

In Regency London's glittering ballrooms, a well-made match can mean the difference between power and ruin.

London, 1813: With his reputation and inheritance on the

line, Lord Percy is determined to win the heart of the coveted diamond of the season. When that beautiful woman vanishes, his failure seems all but certain.

Unless, that is, he can find her.

Lady Grace is devastated when her best friend disappears. Society may be willing to believe the worst, but Grace knows her friend would never run off without leaving her a clue.

Someone kidnapped her - but who?

With the clock ticking, Lord Percy and Lady Grace find their best hope lies in working together. But strong wills, brash decisions, and pesky sparks aren't the only things standing in their way.

Can they trust each other in a society where people will do anything to rise to the top?

Find out in **The Missing Diamond**. Order your copy now on Amazon.

* * *

Want more Dora and Rex? They will be back in **Murder in the House**.

A death in the House of Commons has all eyes on foreign shores. But what if the killer lies closer to home?

London, 1924. Westminster is in an uproar when a promising young clerk is found dead at his desk, killed by a powerful poison sent by post. Worse yet, the letter was addressed to his boss - the Leader of the House.

Dora and Rex, with the help of Clark and Prudence, must determine who sent the killer letter and why. Between political parties jostling for power and enemies plotting overseas, there is no shortage of suspects.

Can the bright young foursome find the killer before he strikes again?

Find out in **Murder in the House**. Order your copy now on Amazon.

* * *

Want to keep updated on my newest books? Subscribe to my newsletter for book news, sales, special offers, and great reading recommendations. You can sign up here: lynnmorrison. myflodesk.com/dcd-newsletter

Historical Notes

When I began writing this series, I had no specific plans for any of the secondary characters. I had no idea Inga and Harris would want to marry, nor that Inga would get Dora to the altar as well. I certainly did not foresee Clark sticking around past book one. As for Lord Audley, while writing The Missing Agent, I decided his wife was dead. That thought planted a seed that finally bloomed in this book.

Writing the story of Lady Audley's demise gave me the excuse to delve back into an earlier time period. I cracked open my history books to find relevant matters of foreign and domestic policy in which Lord Audley and Lord Cavendish might have been involved. I touched lightly on the Spanish American War and the renewed lease of Hong Kong. The more interesting tidbit to me, however, was the story of the dollar princesses.

As an avid fan of Downton Abbey, I had some notion of Americans coming over to wed into the British upper class. But I had little clue just how widespread a phenomenon it was, nor how close to my physical home it would hit. I had only to travel down the road to Blenheim Palace to find my first example in

Consuelo Vanderbilt. As I said in the book, she married the Duke of Marlborough, providing him with the funds to save the Blenheim Estate. The money was not enough to ensure a stunning relationship between the pair.

If you would like to know more about Consuelo and the dollar princess lifestyle, you can read her own words in her book The Glitter and the Gold (by Consuelo Vanderbilt Balsan).

As always, I sought to add in a few period-specific individuals, including famed Bright Young Thing photographer Cecil Beaton. If Clark's scavenger hunt had truly taken place, I have little doubt that Beaton would have captured it for posterity. His career spanned five decades, and included everyone from the Bright Young Things to the royal family to Hollywood's A list. You can see a wide selection of his photography on Artnet (https://www.artnet.com/artists/cecil-beaton).

Two years ago, I made a very quick trip to The American Bar at the Savoy Hotel. It was late in the evening and the bar was preparing to close. I managed little more than to stick my head in the front room, but that was enough to catch my interest. As an American living in England, I couldn't help but wonder how the bar came by its name. Imagine my delight when I discovered it was named for the types of cocktails it served rather than because it was a watering hole for American expats. (Although, I am sure plenty visited, especially during the Roaring 20s.) With prohibition going on across the pond, the American cocktail masters travelled overseas to share their knowledge with a willing audience. They made it to more than England. I am currently sitting in Venice, Italy, where earlier this week I stumbled upon another American Bar in one of Venice's famed calle. I was very pleased to announce I knew where it got its name. My children, unfortunately, showed no interest in learning about the topic. Such is life with teenagers!

Murder in the House
A Dora and Rex 1920s Mystery

A death in the House of Commons has all eyes on foreign shores. But what if the killer lies closer to home?

London, 1924. Westminster is in an uproar when a promising young clerk is found dead at his desk, killed by a powerful poison sent by post. Worse yet, the letter was addressed to his boss - the Leader of the House.

Dora and Rex, with the help of Clark and Prudence, must determine who sent the killer letter and why. Between political parties jostling for power and enemies plotting overseas, there is no shortage of suspects.

Can the bright young foursome find the killer before he strikes again?

Find out in Murder in the House. Order your copy now.

The Missing Diamond
A Crown Jewels Regency Mystery

In Regency London's glittering ballrooms, a well-made match can mean the difference between power and ruin.

London, 1813: With his reputation and inheritance on the line, Lord Percy is determined to win the heart of the coveted diamond of the season. When that beautiful woman vanishes, his failure seems all but certain.

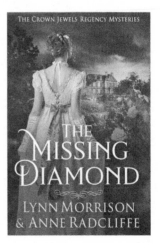

Unless, that is, he can find her.

Lady Grace is devastated when her best friend disappears. Society may be willing to believe the worst, but Grace knows her friend would never run off without leaving her a clue.

Someone kidnapped her - but who?

With the clock ticking, Lord Percy and Lady Grace find their best hope lies in working together. But strong wills, brash decisions, and pesky sparks aren't the only things standing in their way.

Can they trust each other in a society where people will do anything to rise to the top?

Find out in **The Missing Diamond**. Order your copy now on Amazon.

Acknowledgments

As always, Ken Morrison and Anne Radcliffe remained on hand to unravel my plot knots and pull me from blind alleys. Thank you for always being there for me!

I very much appreciate the time and effort my beta readers Brenda Chapman and Anne Kavcic put into giving my books a first full read. They point out all the plot holes so I can sew them up before release.

Thanks to my ARC team for helping get out the word about my books.

A final huge thanks to you, my readers! So many of you lend me support via email or comments in my Facebook group. I never ever feel like I am in this alone.

About the Author

Lynn Morrison lives in Oxford, England along with her husband, two daughters and two cats. Born and raised in Mississippi, her wanderlust attitude has led her to live in California, Italy, France, the UK, and the Netherlands. Despite having rubbed shoulders with presidential candidates and members of parliament, night-clubbed in Geneva and Prague, explored Japanese temples and scrambled through Roman ruins, Lynn's real life adventures can't compete with the stories in her mind.

She is as passionate about reading as she is writing, and can almost always be found with a book in hand. You can find out more about her on her website LynnMorrisonWriter.com.

You can chat with her directly in her Facebook group - Lynn Morrison's Not a Book Club - where she talks about books, life and anything else that crosses her mind.

facebook.com/nomadmomdiary

instagram.com/nomadmomdiary

bookbub.com/authors/lynn-morrison

goodreads.com/nomadmomdiary

amazon.com/Lynn-Morrison/e/BooIKC1LVW

Also by Lynn Morrison

Fangs & Cauldrons

Made in United States
Orlando, FL
17 April 2024

45891547R00129